D0407747

· An ·

Underground Railroad Diary

JERDINE NOLEN

•

A Paula Wiseman Book
Simon & Schuster Books for Young Readers

•

New York London Toronto Sydney

To Paula Wiseman, wise woman
and editor for the journey

Please note that for the sake of the overall story, in the Governor Hunt reference on page 28, I write that this article was written in 1854. E. D. Morgan was only in office as a New York state senator until 1853. The actual letter was written in 1852.

SIMON & SCHUSTER BOOKS FOR YOUNG READERS
An imprint of Simon & Schuster Children's Publishing Division
1230 Avenue of the Americas, New York, New York 10020

Book design by Krista Vossen
Quilt illustration by Shadra Strickland
Map illustration by Drew Willis
The text for this book is set in Apolline.
Manufactured in the United States of America
1211 FFG
2 4 6 8 10 9 7 5 3 1
Library of Congress Cataloging-in-Publication Data
Nolen, Jerdine.
Eliza's freedom road : an Underground Railroad diary / Jerdine Nolen. — 1st ed.
p. cm.
"A Paula Wiseman Book."
Summary: A twelve-year-old slave girl begins writing in a journal where she documents her journey via the Underground Railroad from Alexandria, Virginia to freedom in St. Catharines, Canada.
Summary: Includes bibliographical references (p. 147–150).
ISBN 978-1-4169-5814-7 (hardcover)
[1. Slavery—Fiction. 2. Underground Railroad—Fiction. 3. Fugitive slaves—Fiction. 4. African Americans—Fiction. 5. Diaries—Fiction.]
I. Title.
PZ7.H23125El 2011
[Fic]—dc22
2010020931
ISBN 978-1-4424-1723-6 (eBook)

"A . . . MIND LOVES STORIES FROM OF OLD,

BEING THE KIND IT CAN REPEAT AND HOLD."

—FROM CHAUCER, "THE PARDONER'S TALE,"
THE CANTERBURY TALES

ACKNOWLEDGMENTS

A hearty thank-you to the kind and loving staff at the Writers' Colony at Dairy Hollow in Eureka Springs, Arkansas, for providing a cocoon that helped me launch my dream, Eliza's journey.

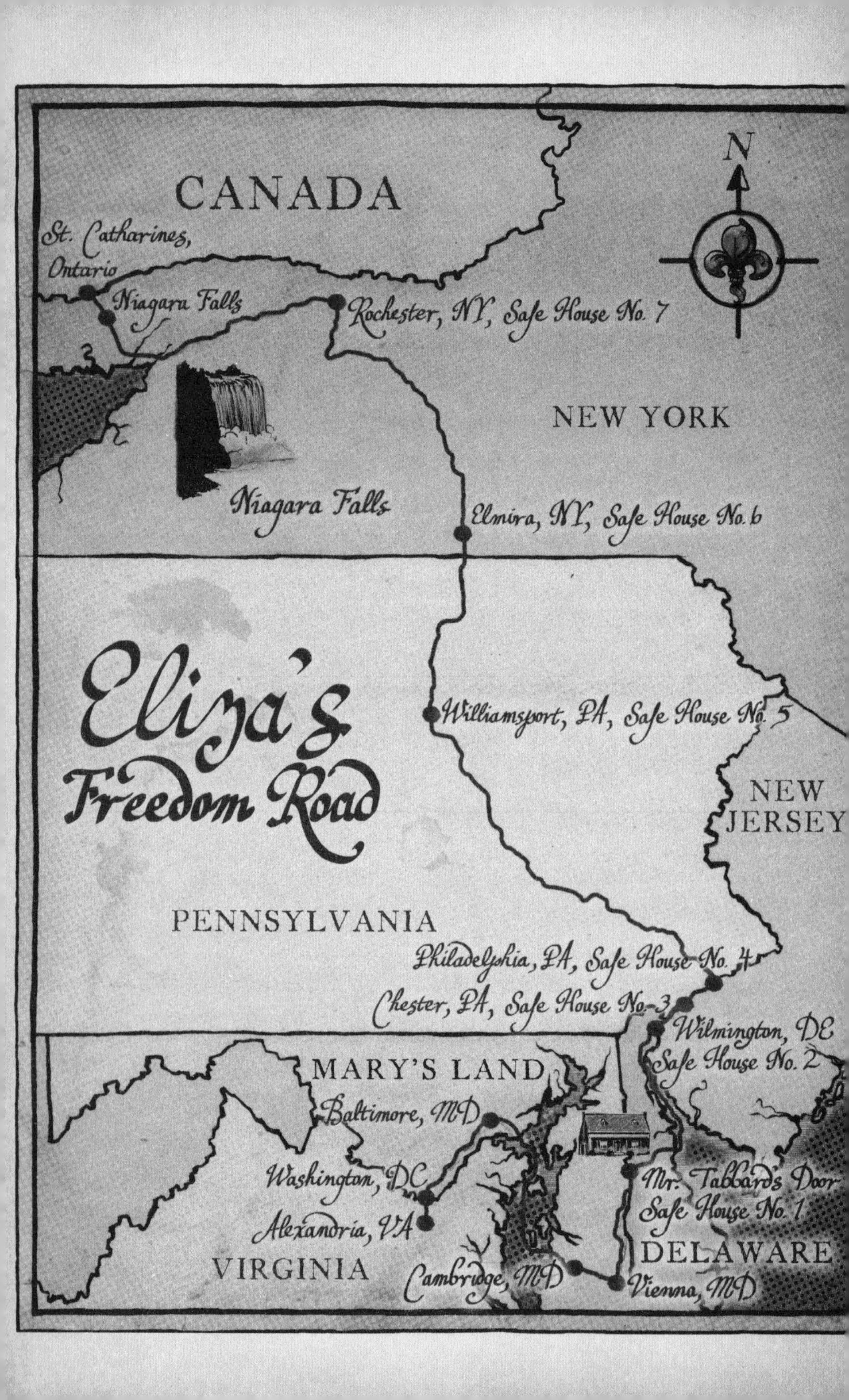
CANADA
N
St. Catharines, Ontario
Niagara Falls
Rochester, NY, Safe House No. 7
NEW YORK
Niagara Falls
Elmira, NY, Safe House No. 6
Eliza's Freedom Road
Williamsport, PA, Safe House No. 5
NEW JERSEY
PENNSYLVANIA
Philadelphia, PA, Safe House No. 4
Chester, PA, Safe House No. 3
Wilmington, DE Safe House No. 2
MARY'S LAND
Baltimore, MD
Washington, DC
Mr. Tabbard's Door Safe House No. 1
Alexandria, VA
DELAWARE
VIRGINIA
Cambridge, MD
Vienna, MD

PROLOGUE

January 1, 1867
Rochester, New York

Dear Reader,

I am Eliza. Not the girl, but the grown woman Eliza. It has been many years since I was called Eliza. I call myself Elizabeth now. Abbey would say that I am my full self, the one Mistress and Sir should not see. When she told me that, I was only a girl of eleven. As I look back, I see the way things were. I was a Slave then, but I escaped to freedom in Canada.

So much has happened in these years. It was the sixteenth president, Mr. Abraham Lincoln, who said, "If slavery is not wrong, nothing is wrong." And from 1861 to 1865 a War Between the States was fought and won. Now the question of Slavery has been decided upon. In 1863, Mr. Lincoln signed the Emancipation Proclamation abolishing Slavery in these United States. All during those war years, I lived in St. Catharines, Ontario, in Canada. This was where I grew into my free self.

At the age of eleven, I started a diary. In it, I remember the Friends and the events of my escape journey to freedom. Reading my diary, I see that what was not clear to me then is clear to me now. I see the road and the journey, which led to my freedom. This is my record. This was my freedom road. Looking back, I am able to draw the route of my passage. How I wish that my dear Abbey could see that my story has come out just fine.

You may be interested to know how I finished my story. Read on.

Life with Abbey in Virginia

February 6–June 22, 1854

Monday, February 6, 1854
Alexandria, Virginia

I love to work in the kitchen, where I can be close to Abbey. One day I will work alongside her in the kitchen. She will teach me what she knows and I will serve a master and mistress. I do not know what else there is for me.

Abbey is my mistress's cook. Mistress never worries to come to us here. All the time she says she is glad the kitchen is in the kitchen yard away from the house, where it is supposed to be. She does not like the heat or the cooking smells. But I do. I like them most fine.

Abbey is as close to me as a mother, but she is not my mother. My mother is Jane Mae. I never knew my father, but Abbey knows. Abbey says she knows every hair on my head. She was my mother's dearest friend. She was the midwife who brought me into this world. She nursed me back to my health once when I fell so sick. Mistress said the sickness was Shock that came from the suddenness of losing my beloved mother, Jane Mae. Shock sickness is a deep, dark sadness that covers you. Even when the Shock has passed, it never leaves, like the smell from Sir's tobacco smoke.

I love Abbey mightily, for she tells me the things I

need to know to keep me safe. This night, before we slept, I asked her, "Why am I all the time so full up with thoughts and words in my head?"

She did what she always does when she tells me something I need to know. She smiled and patted me. "You got reasons so many talking words in there." Then she tapped my head. Tap, tap, tap. "Your mama filled your head up with stories. And Mistress petted you and taught you to read and to write." Then she said, "Eliza, you are a child who is all filled up with words." I love when Abbey tells me these things. My arms are not long enough to wrap around Abbey's waist like I did with my mother. I wrap my arms tight around Abbey as far as they can go.

Then Abbey told me, "You are not like me, Eliza." First this made me sad. She is all I have now. But my sadness did not linger for long. I became the happiest I can be!

"Talk your words in this," she told me. That's when Abbey gave me Mistress's never-been-used writing diary. Mistress had thrown it out. She cannot see so well to write anymore. I am writing in it now. Abbey gave me two lead pencils, too.

"Write your words in it. But do not ever let Sir see you do it," she warned me. I know what she means. It is unlawful for Slaves to read and write. Mistress does not but Sir enforces the Slave Laws to the letter. Sometimes I am so full of fear for writing in my little book. But I must write. It helps me to think and remember.

Sunday, February 12, 1854
Alexandria, Virginia

All day long I worked beside Abbey cleaning out the kitchen garden. Soon the ground will be warm enough to turn over. When we stopped I asked Abbey, "Tell me your favorite story." But Abbey said, "I cannot tell the stories the way your mother, Jane Mae, did. I never did learn them good enough to tell. I just know them good enough to know." When my mother, Jane Mae, was here, there was always a story to listen to. Back then, Abbey said, "Jane Mae told the stories right, from the old way." Then Abbey did not speak for a long time. Finally she said to me, "Eliza, you should tell the stories now . . . you your mother's daughter. Look at the picture pattern on your quilt, and remember how each one goes." And Abbey said something that made a smile come up. "You already got them inside you." She poked my chest and tapped my head the same way my mother, Jane Mae, did. "Remembering in your head and feeling in your heart tells you you always is loved, Eliza."

Wednesday, February 15, 1854
Alexandria, Virginia

This day brought too many chores. I did all my usual ones. The work was hard but I have strong hands. Every day I carry the firewood to the kitchen. I fetch hot water to fill two tubs for Sir and Mistress to bathe in; I fill a third for them to rinse off in. I do not spill a drop. I broom-sweep the floors. I peel potatoes and empty the rinds. I scour the pots. Then today Mistress said, "Now, Eliza, you must wait on me since Caroline and Abbey cannot." Sir said Abbey and Caroline must help prepare the seed beds for the tobacco. Poor Abbey, she cannot stomach the bad smell from the tobacco, whether it is seedlings or the full-grown plants.

I had to serve Mistress's morning, afternoon, and evening meals in her room. Mistress is not the same, either, since we lost my mother. She was not always so friendly, and now she is much more sickly and more frail. Mistress is beginning to look like one of those long-necked white egret birds with yellow eyes that live at the river. Abbey says Mistress has always been sickly, and sickest in the winter months. Now that things will be warming soon, Abbey says her strength will come all the way back. I hope so; this sickness in her body is causing Mistress's eyes to go blind. Abbey says she reckons there is a whole lot in the world Mistress just don't want to see. I try to understand Abbey, but sometimes what she says is puzzlement to me. Still, Abbey said she would teach me to gather the herb from the forest and prepare the all-heal remedy. But I already know this. I want to tell Abbey I know where to find the best all-heal. Mama always said it is best for Mistress's ailments where it is wild in the deep woods. All my life my mother would take me to the woods with her to gather it. She taught me about plants and these things and what to do if I am ever lost in the woods. I will wait until Abbey's mind is eased from working with tobacco to remind her of this.

Monday, February 20, 1854
Alexandria, Virginia

This morning Sir said Abbey must do more tobacco. This makes her very vexed on Sir. She never wants to be around tobacco. When Abbey is most vexed on Sir, she speaks her mind to me. Today she said there is something I must know and always remember. I write it here so I will never forget. "The Slave has to be two of they selves. One self belongs to Mistress and Sir. The other one belongs to you, Eliza." Then she tapped my chest. "Keep that one hid. Do not ever let Sir see that one. Do not ever let Sir know that Eliza is even alive." Abbey told me this so I can stay safe. Some of us are beaten, sold, or more—much worse, than those who do not do this. And now, for the first time, my eyes are all the way open. I can see for myself what this is meaning.

This day Caroline's oldest boy, Abel, was sold away. I have heard Sir say all the time to Mistress, "That boy do not know his place." Early this morning Caroline came to Sir crying. She begged Sir, "Oh, Master, please do not take my boy from me!" When Sir turned a deaf ear to her, she ran after the wagon. But before she could catch it, Mr. Forrnistock, the overseer, caught up to her on his horse. He landed three heavy blows across her shoulders with his piece of rawhide strap. She dropped to her knees crying. Then they dragged her off to her cabin. No telling how long she will be down from the Shock sick.

This filled me up with such fear. What will Sir think of me one day? I said this to Abbey. But Abbey said the mistress would protect me. My head wonders why Mistress would save me and not my beloved mother, Jane Mae? I know Abbey did all she could.

Tuesday, February 21, 1854
Alexandria, Virginia

Today my head is full of remembering. Caroline's Shock sickness made me remember my own. But Abbey says the past must stay the past. I try but the remembering keeps coming to the front of my mind. I think of that day Sir sold my mother away from here. Abbey said that was a mean trick Sir played on me.

Early that morning Sir had called for me. "Eliza, you go on to town with Ezekiel." *Me?* I thought. Sir had never sent me to town with Ezekiel to get supplies before, even though I always wanted to go. Ezekiel always goes to town for Sir. He cares for the horses and carriages, too. At first I thought maybe Sir was turning nice, but there was no smile in his voice and his hard face looked about the same.

The sun was high and pretty in that bright blue sky. The way we go to town, we must pass the whitewash building. "That is the Slave pen," Ezekiel said of the place where slaves come to wait to be sold. Ezekiel knows all about it. He talked and talked of it but I hummed so I did not have to hear.

When we came back from town, I carried a peppermint sweet in the hem of my skirt so it would not melt all the way from Mr. Riley's store. Mrs. Riley had gave two to me. I ate one; the other peppermint was to be a present to my mother. Sir disallows us to have pockets.

I ran from the wagon to the kitchen before Ezekiel had time to unload. I wanted to see my mother's face full of love. But I did not see her face at all. She was not in the kitchen yard. She was not in the kitchen. She was not tending Mistress. She was not where she was supposed to be with Abbey. It was just a mournful Abbey in the kitchen, stirring tears into Sir's stew. My mother was nowhere that I could find her. Then Abbey told me what had happened. "Jane Mae is gone. Sir sold her off." I know Sir probably sent her to the whitewash pen that Ezekiel showed me. I started to run there, but Ezekiel caught me. That's all I remember, before I fell down sick.

That day, Abbey said Sir is not for truth. He speaks lies. He separates us and sells us away when he says he will not. Abbey said Sir is the worst of a master. Abbey tried to soothe me with her words. But it is not words that I wanted. It was my mother. For how long I was down, I do not know. But when I awoke, Abbey and Mistress were at my side. Mistress said Abbey doctored me back to myself. When I think on this, it makes my sadness deep as the river. I do not want to be by myself all alone in the world without my mother, Jane Mae. Abbey said nobody slept well in the house for two days. Sir said Abbey put too much salt in his stew. He had a stomachache for a week. Mistress cried steadily. She loved my mother best. That was nearly about one year ago now.

The day I woke up, Abbey was still crying. I remembered my mother's voice, it saying, "Be careful, my daughter, Eliza. But do not fear. You will never be lost from me." And then I remembered what Ezekiel said: "Be like me, Eliza, and forget you even had a mama." But I knew I could not do that. I will not do that. And now that I have my little writing book, I can remember everything about Mama. And like Abbey says, I can remember her stories because they are inside me now. I will write them in my little book to remember them always. This is my favorite one:

Each day as the sun rose, a man set out to hunt. And every evening as the sun went down, he returned to his home and family with the prize of his hunt.

One day the man did not return. Another day came and another night went, but the man did not return. A week went by, then a month. About the seventh month, the seventh son was born to the man and his wife. His name was Asa. The boy grew in a fine way. There came a time when Asa began to talk. The first thing he said was "Where is my papa?"

"Yes," said the eldest son. "Where is our papa?"

"He should have come back a long time ago," said the second son.

"Something must have happened," said the third.

"I saw him go toward the village," said the fourth son.

"I saw him go across the river," said the fifth.

"We should follow his footsteps to see if they will lead us to him," said the sixth son.

They walked deep into the forest. Finally they came to a clearing. There on the ground were the man's bones and rusted spear. Now they knew what had happened to him.

The first son stepped forward and said, "I know how to put bones together." He put them together, each in the right place.

The second son said, "I know how to cover the bones with flesh." He covered the bones just as they should be.

The third son said, "I have the power to make blood flow through his veins."

The fourth son said, "I can put back breath into his body."

The fifth son said, "I can give the power to move." Sure enough the man opened his eyes. He stretched. He sat upright.

"I can give the power of speech," said the sixth son, and he did. The man had to do the rest on his own.

When it was all right, Asa hugged his papa for the first time.

"It is time to go home," the man said to his sons.

The man's wife was most overjoyed to see her husband again. "Something must be done to show how grateful we are to have you back in the land of the living," she said.

In thanks the man killed one of his best cows. There was a great feast for all in the village. Then he took the tail of the cow and braided it. He decorated it with beads and cowry shells. It was a fine and beautiful cow-tail switch. Everyone admired it. The man said, "I will give it away to the one who did the most for me to bring me back to the land of the living."

The first son said, "I am oldest; give it to me."

The second son said, "I deserve it more."

The third son said, "I should not be left out."

The fourth son said, "Surely I deserve it."

The fifth son stood. "My gift was best."

The sixth son said, "I should have the cow-tail switch."

The man thought, but he did not think for long. "I have decided," he said. "I will give it to Asa because he did the most. He was the one who asked: 'Where is my papa?' You see, a person is dead only when he is truly forgotten."

I know I could never do what Ezekiel said. I will always remember I have a mother and her name is Jane Mae.

Sunday, February 26, 1854
Alexandria, Virginia

Today Sir was on the warpath. He made me so full of fear. When it was time to sleep Abbey asked me how come I do not write in my little book? I told her I have nothing to say to it. Abbey knows me better than that. She said, "You remember Sir is early to bed and late to rise, Eliza. These are two good times that Sir would not even pay attention to you." Now I see I have so much to say. And the fear of Sir does not keep me from remembering in my little book, and I feel so much freer to write.

Wednesday, March 1, 1854
Alexandria, Virginia

I am Eliza. It is shortened for Elizabeth. Come April and this spring, I am to be twelve years old. Abbey will drop another pebble in a jar for every year of my life. Then all the year long she will have me count them again and again. I know that twelve comes after eleven the same way I know I am always hungry. Abbey saves what she can for me. But today Abbey said in time the hunger I feel should be for more than food. "It should be for your freedom." "Freedom" is a big-sounding word but I did not say this to Abbey. Then Abbey spooned a crumb of bread pudding into my mouth before she popped the pan onto the floor of the oven. I love the word that says "Abbey's bread pudding." I could eat that all day. I spelled it in flour on the baking table:

ABBEY'S BREAD PUDDING.

Abbey clicked her tongue. "Yes," she said, brushing the words away. "Soon and very soon you be grown too big for this kitchen. Take a paper and write down this recipe. Your mama loved this on a cool night, and you should make it for your little ones one day."

Abbey's Bread Pudding

Cut or break one loaf of stale bread into fine pieces and sprinkle with a little salt. Take a pint of cream and a quarter of a pound of butter, set it on the fire, and keep it stirring; when the butter is melted, put in the bread pieces. Cover until cool and well soaked; mash it well. Beat six eggs very light, powdered nutmeg and cinnamon, and a half cupful of sugar. Mix it all together, butter a dish, put it in, and bake it in a quick oven, one hour and a half.

It made me happy to have a favorite of Mama's so close by in my diary.

Sunday, April 2, 1854
Alexandria, Virginia

It is all the way April now. I am living twelve years. This is one whole year without my mother.

Today I have only my mother's memory and the stories she would tell. This makes me feel as if a deep well inside me cannot be filled. I said to my mind that something inside me is lost. Then, somewhere else in me, I heard the little song Mama always hummed to me. I cannot sing out loud how it goes.

Thursday, April 6, 1854
Alexandria, Virginia

The only keepsake of my mother is this quilt that covers me. She stitched it with her very hands. When I was small she would wrap me up tight inside it. Then she would tell me such wondrous stories. She would laugh and say to me, *Eliza, did I ever tell you about the time . . . ?*

All my years she said to me, "Eliza, this is your story quilt. I made it special for you so you can remember the stories, too!" Everyone always wanted to hear Mama tell stories. I even remember Mistress asked for special ones sometimes. She even said to my mother, "Jane Mae, you are a natural storyteller."

My quilt has twelve panels. Each panel is stitched to show a picture pattern of a story she would tell to me. She did this so I could remember the stories. If I close my eyes I can describe the pictures without even looking. Nobody knows I remember all of Jane Mae's stories, but especially the ones on my story quilt.

The first picture pattern is stitched with the cow-tail switch decorated with buttons and beads and shiny thread. In the second panel is stitched many shades of blue for the water and the sky; the white is for the wind. My favorite spider story is in the third panel. Then, in the fourth panel, two people and every kind of bird have taken to the air and are flying.

The second row starts with panel number five. A proud rooster with his big red comb and colorful feathers sits high up in a tree. He is looking down at sly-looking, hungry-looking, bushy-tailed Mr. Reynard Fox. Night as deep and dark as velvet in the sixth panel is filled with the sun, moon, and many shining stars, including the North Star. Here Mama stitched into the quilt a gadget called a compass. It always points to the north.

Long-eared Brother Rabbit running fast away from bushy-tailed Brother Wolf is in panel number seven. The wisest man in the whole Bible, Moses, is parting open the sea in the eighth panel. Then, in panel number nine, all you can see of the shepherd boy David is his slingshot. And all you can see of Goliath are his legs because he is so big and tall—he is a giant. Panel number ten has a little man sitting up in a tree with Mr. Owl. Panels eleven and twelve are not filled yet. Mama said they are for my stories, for me to sew one day. But I do not know how yet. Mama said, "Eliza, you got time yet. Just remember, a good story is how it comes out at the end.

"Maybe," she said, "your stories will come out in freedom. Just because you are born in Slavery does not mean you have to stay there." I remember that Mama said that to me over and often, just the way Abbey now says it.

Friday, April 7, 1854
Alexandria, Virginia

Tomorrow, Abbey said, we shall plant the kitchen garden.

Saturday, April 8, 1854
Alexandria, Virginia

Today was setting-out day. This is Sir's happiest time. Tobacco plants must be placed in the ground while the weather is cool and wet. This is very rainy season, so there will be no chance the plants will dry out. Sir said Abbey must work with the tobacco today, not plant the kitchen garden.

Late in the night I awoke from a dream hearing the sound of my mother's voice. The tobacco planting took all day and into the night. Abbey was not here in the room where she should have been sleeping. She was very tired, but the morning meal had to be ready to serve when Mistress rose. I went to help her side by side like Mama would have. "Tell me my favorite one," Abbey said. And I write her story this way, exactly as Mama told it:

Mothers love their children. Back at the beginning of the world Mother Water and Mother Wind used to be friends. One day they got to talking about their children. "I got all kinds of children," Mother Water said. "I got the biggest and the littlest children. I got children of every color. I got children of every kind and shape in the whole world. I love all my children."

Then Mother Wind took a turn. "I love my children, too. I got more children than anybody in the whole wide world. They can move every which way. They fly. They walk. They run. They swim. They sing. They talk. They whistle and they cry. Lord oh Lord, my children sure are a pleasure to me. Nobody in the whole wide world has babies like mine." Sooner than soon Mother Water got tired of hearing about Mother Wind's children.

One day the whole passel of Mother Wind's young'uns come up to her. "Mother, we thirsty as we can be. We run and we walk. We fly and we swim. We talk and we sing. We whistle and cry and laugh this whole world through and through."

"Run over to Mother Water to ask for a long cool drink." But Mother Water was churned and stirred up. She grabbed on to every one of them children of wind and would not let go even when Mother Wind called them to come home. Woooooo wooooo woooooooooo. *Mother Wind passed over the ocean, calling her children. But every time she called, there was only a rustle of an answer—a white feathery cap came up to the top of the water. Time and time again no wind children, only white*

feathery caps. When Mother Water did not show up to talk anymore, Mother Wind knew what had happened. Mother Wind never saw her children again. Mama says that is why the wind sounds so lonesome sometimes. But she still calls for them. She is still looking for her children to come on home. Mothers love their children.

Yesterday Abbey told me, "You surely are Jane Mae's daughter. You got the stories in you, all right." I hope she is right.

Sunday, April 9, 1854
Alexandria, Virginia

This morning Abbey told me I must wait on Mistress the whole day. I do not mind to do this one bit because Sir is called away today. Everything is grim when he is near.

Monday, April 10, 1854
Alexandria, Virginia

I am very busy with Mistress now. I help with everything. This is what I must do: First I help Mistress rise. Then, I wash her, get her dressed, comb her hair, and make sure she eats breakfast, supper, and dinner. Today Mistress said she feels strong, but to me she does not look it. Some days she is hardly able to feed herself. I help guide her spoon into her mouth so the food does not go on her dress or the floor.

Abbey says to mind when I am around Sir and Mistress. I do. Sir is back today. Today Mistress talked to Sir like I was not there. She said she is not sad the Good Lord did not bless them with children to depend on. Then Sir said that is what the Slave is for. I declare, when Sir said this, everything inside me went cold like leftover porridge. I declare I find what Mistress says most curious. I remember her telling Mama so many times how she wished she had had at least one child to depend on and to love.

I think inside myself how I wish I could be for only myself and not for Sir at all and only *sometimes* for Mistress when she is not having one of her angry, hateful spells. Abbey said Mistress was kind before she got so sick.

Thursday, April 13, 1854
Alexandria, Virginia

Now my mistress needs me so. When my mother was here, she served *only* Mistress. Then Caroline.

Now it is my job. But Mistress was not ailing the way she ails now. Abbey said to mind and watch how she prepares the all-heal medicine she gives to her. One day it will be my turn to make it for her. This night while Mistress was deep in sleep, I rose, for there was too much light coming from that full moon. I look out the window and what do I see? The North Star is twinkling just as bright.

Saturday, April 15, 1854
Alexandria, Virginia

Normal times I sleep on my pallet, a mattress filled with straw and corn husks in the loft of the storeroom near Abbey or close by the fire in the kitchen. I am first to rise to start the fire so it is hot for her. I sweep the ash to the side to get ready to bake the morning bread. I fetch water and firewood for cooking. I scrub pots. I peel potatoes and tend the kitchen garden—whatever Abbey needs. Times are not normal now.

I sleep on a bed that rolls out from underneath my mistress's bed. That way I am close when she calls for me, which is oftener and oftener by the day and the night. This means I cannot write much. This bed is soft but there is no comfort here. I long to be in the kitchen next to Abbey.

Tuesday, April 18, 1854
Alexandria, Virginia

Today, most of this day Mistress wanted to hear me read to her from the Good Book.

I love to read the Good Book. I read: *The Lord is my shepherd; I shall not want. He maketh me to lie down in green pastures: he leadeth me beside the still waters. He restoreth my soul: he leadeth me in the paths of righteousness for his name's sake.* When I told Abbey what I read today and how much I love these words, she said the next best green pastures there ever were is in freedom.

Wednesday, April 19, 1854
Alexandria, Virginia

How lucky I am to be able to read! Sometimes I read out loud all the morning long to Mistress. At first this gives me a scare to be so bold to read in front of Sir, too. I asked Abbey what I'm afraid to say to Mistress: Why won't she read for herself? She loves to read. She is a good reader. She taught me how to read. She gave me her old childhood hornbook to practice my letters and verse. Every day she did this when Mama was here and times were so much better than this. Now Abbey says Mistress is nearly all the way blind.

Sunday, April 30, 1854
Alexandria, Virginia

Now I also read from the newspaper. And there is so much news.

This is a Bad News, Bad Luck Day. Today I read to Mistress from the newspaper about what happened yesterday, when the ground moved and my heart trembled so. Yesterday there was an earthquake. I thought the whole world was coming to an end. Mistress screamed and cried when her looking glass mirror fell to the floor and cracked all to pieces. I fear this may add to her bad luck. Part of the chimney fell to the ground and now must be repaired. Sir cussed something awful. Abbey said that it means something when the earth shakes and quakes. It means change is coming. Where the earth quakes, the ground where you walked will never walk the same. "You must keep yourself under close watch and mind what you say and do," she said. I declare sometimes what Abbey says frightens me so.

Then this same day there is worse bad news for Abbey and me. I read in the newspaper today: "A Negro Arrested and Shot, whether by accident or design we cannot say. A Negro named Smith was shot while in custody. A number of blacks were present when it happened." I was so afraid for myself but I did not let it show.

Sunday, May 14, 1854
Alexandria, Virginia

Good news today for me, because Slaves have escaped their bonds. This is not good news for Sir. This is what the paper said: "More Fugitive Slaves. Warrants have been issued today for the arrest of several fugitive slaves in Rochester, New York. Three slaves have known to have been in the city yesterday, but they are believed to have taken a sudden departure by the underground railroad, and there is little prospect of any arrest."

Do they mean departure by an underground railroad train? Is there a way they escaped on a train that runs under the ground? I want to know how to find that train station. I want to know how to get three tickets: one for Abbey, one for Mama, one for me. Abbey hushed me. Do not talk about such things out loud, she said. Tonight, I tell these things to the moon, which is glowing so bright, and my star.

I declare, I love to read to my mistress but sometimes it gives me too much fear of what I know.

Saturday, May 20, 1854
Alexandria, Virginia

Mistress is getting stronger now. Abbey said I must make the all-heal remedy. It will work, but slowly. Mistress is still very low and sickly.

This morning when Mistress woke she did not want to rise. She felt strong but she only wanted to hear me read. “Read the Good Book to me, Eliza. Read me the Genesis story,” she said. I started the reading looking at the book. I read: “In the beginning.” I read the rest from my heart without looking at the words. Abbey said this is my gift.

Tuesday, May 23, 1854
Alexandria, Virginia

Today I snuck to find Abbey while Mistress slept. I told her about my day. Then I rushed right back to Mistress’s bedside before she woke.

Later while I was reading the newspaper to my mistress, I thought how lucky I am to know how to read. And I think of this even while I have to read all the horrible stories from the newspaper. Sir said Mistress must know these things that happen in the world. He said, “The master must be vigilant over his Slaves.”

One thing unsettles me so. It says in three months' time there is to be another Slave sale auction. That means August. Maybe in August Sir will send me to the whitewash pen and sell me away. I pray not, only if he will tell me whre he has sent my mother.

I wonder to Abbey if Sir could buy my mother back like he say he will. Abbey said Sir cannot bring her back till he pays off his debt. By the time he can pay it off, no telling where my mother will be. First she was sold to a farm in Natchez, Mississippi. Now word has come that she was sold to a farm somewhere in Kentucky. I asked Abbey if she thinks I will ever see my mother again but she has no answer for me.

Wednesday, May 24, 1854
Alexandria, Virginia

Sir was angry as can be today. He cusses too much for Mistress's taste. Today he cussed because of the poster paper of a wanted fugitive runaway. There is a reward for the capture of the woman. No Slave catcher knows how to capture her. Sir said to Mistress he wants to catch her with his bare hands. I prayed so hard in my heart he does not ever catch her or any other runaway. I prayed she can take the underground railroad train or follow the North

Star. Mama said to always keep it over your left shoulder and the river on your right side.

Thursday, May 25, 1854
Alexandria, Virginia

Today I read this in the paper: "Governor Hunt on the fugitive pardon. Governor Hunt has deemed it proper to notice in a letter to Senator E. D. Morgan that the case of SNOWDEN, a colored convict and a fugitive slave, recently was pardoned out of the Sing Sing prison.

I am glad of this news. I wonder if they sent him on the underground train to his freedom?

Sunday, May 28, 1854
Alexandria, Virginia

Today Sir was *so* vexed. It does not matter that it is the Sabbath. All morning he cussed and yelled at us and then at Mistress. But I thought he yelled the worst to Mistress. So many times today I heard Mistress say to Sir how she mightily needs me. Then Sir said something to her in a bad, bad voice—more bad than he say to us. I did not make out the words. But I know it is because I read out in the open to my mistress and write for her and I am a Slave. Sir said he *must* enforce the Slave Laws to the letter. But on this matter Mistress does not. Abbey said Sir was not so harsh toward Mistress before she turned sick. To hear Mistress crying so makes me feel a deep well of sadness for her and fear for Abbey and me.

Wednesday, May 31, 1854
Alexandria, Virginia

Late in the day, a man came to see Sir. When I passed through the parlor I heard him say something to Sir about the price I would fetch. I pretended I did not hear the talk. But I am in so much fear. Soon as I could, I ran to Abbey's apron. "Something must happen to save me," I cried to her. But we do not know what it can be.

Thursday, June 1, 1854
Alexandria, Virginia

This morning Dr. Hardy came to give Mistress a bleeding cure. He says getting rid of the bad blood is a good way to heal my mistress. He uses his little old leeches that he said he loves, which come all the way from France! I must do what he says, but it is the worst thing. I have to hand him the precious leeches when he calls for them. I do, but I put my mind someplace else because I do not like these things. He put seven of them on Mistress's back. After he finished, he turned to me. "Now, Eliza, you must feed your mistress good meals and make sure she rests." When she is up to it, he said a change of scene would do her a world of good.

Mistress slept for a long time. She woke me up in the middle of the night. "Eliza, you must write a letter." This one goes to Mary's Land. Mistress has a sister, Susan, there. Mistress asked one thing: "May I visit very soon?" Then I wrote what Doc Hardy said: a change of scene will do some good.

I could hardly hold the pen to write the letter for fear. If Mistress goes away from me, I think come August, Sir will say my time has come to be sold away from here, too, as he did my poor mother. The Slave sale auction is in two calendar pages away. That is in two months.

Saturday, June 3, 1854
Alexandria, Virginia

Abbey says the sickness takes all of poor Mistress's strength. I try my hardest to please her so she will remember to protect me. But today she was in her hateful mood. "Eliza, I taught you to talk and to read and write the right way. It is a gift to know these things." She looked toward me but she did not see me. "But it is my gift for me because I own you, Eliza. You belong to me!"

"Yes'm," I said. But I believe what Abbey tells me. It is *my* true gift.

Friday, June 9, 1854
Alexandria, Virginia

Today my spirit rose a bit. It is because of Abbey. I visited her in the kitchen while Mistress slept. Abbey said, "I love to hear you talk." She said all my reading and writing and speaking practice improves me. She said I speak so much like our mistress. "Your mother would be proud to know you are growing into a fine-sounding lady." When Abbey says these things, I can see my own mother's face smiling at me.

Monday, June 12, 1854
Alexandria, Virginia

Mistress rose today feeling very hearty. She feels strong enough to take an overnight riding visit to

Simmons Farm with Sir. She will not come back until Sunday. Now I am free to be with Abbey, to return to the kitchen chores and to my corn-husk pallet. I do not have to serve my mistress. I should be happy but I am not; things are not the same. And I think Abbey is right—since the earthquake, the ground does not walk right. I do my best to be of help to Abbey but I dropped the soup pot and spilled all the soup. "Never you mind," Abbey said. "It is not right having a fine-sounding lady doing kitchen chores." My mind wonders, *What am I to do?* Too many worries fill my head.

A Journey Far from Home

June 30–July 20, 1854

Friday, June 30, 1854
Alexandria, Virginia

Everything is changing fast. Mistress is going traveling. For how long I do not know. She is going to visit her sister, Mistress Susan, in Mary's Land. And Mistress said I must accompany her. I ran to Abbey, but Abbey said, "Listen to your mistress. She is right in this."

Mistress's eyesight has gone from bad to worse. Doc Hardy gave her dark spectacles to wear because the bright sunlight hurts her eyes. His bleeding cures do not help that. She cried when she told Sir that she needs my eyes to see for her. Sir hardly seemed to listen to her. I thought maybe I would have good traveling clothes, but I do not. Sir told Mistress to give me an itchy woolsey sack dress to wear. This marks me a Slave.

Again I woke to the big, wide shining moon. I am grateful not to be without Mistress, but what will I do without Abbey?

Thursday, July 6, 1854
Alexandria, Virginia

With each day closer to the journey, Sir's spirit is more and more vexed. I filled up with hope to leave to get away from Sir, but I know I will worry and worry about Abbey. She says not to worry on her because he will not send her away, for he loves her cooking.

How will I live with Abbey so far away? I miss her just thinking about leaving. Abbey told me Mary's Land is farther north, that means closer toward freedom than Virginia.

Thursday, July 13, 1854
Alexandria, Virginia

I'm not so sure Doc Hardy is right. Mistress progresses but it is not steady. But Doc Hardy says the precious little leeches have worked. Still, Abbey told me I must continue giving Mistress the all-heal. Some days Mistress feels strong and high like her spirit is up in the trees; other days she is low to the ground. On the good days she sings. Singing makes everybody happy, but not Sir. But Abbey said some people are rotten to the core and are not meant to be happy.

Sunday, July 16, 1854
Alexandria, Virginia

While I was packing my mistress's trunks, Sir came to her room. He stood before me so I could not get by.

"Eliza, where do you think you are going?" Sir said, sounding too big for his own words.

"Getting ready to journey with Mistress," I said, well as I can.

"And who gave you permission?" he asked, almost as a shout.

"My mistress," I was careful to say. *Surely,* my mind said, *Sir knows this.*

"Oh, perhaps Mistress did mention that to me," he growled, angry like a bear.

He gave his hard look and warning. "Be on your best, Eliza. Do what you are told. Look and speak to no one, only your mistress. If I find you have done otherwise, upon your return, you will regret it more than you know!"

"Yes, sir," I told him, and I nodded. Then I did something I may be whipped for. I am twelve and should know better. I looked at Sir in his eyes. Why did I do this? Sir has hard, gray, cold eyes. Abbey said a Slave must never look at the master this way. Quickly I looked at his boots. I think I am to be whipped for sure.

I am feeling so much fear now. Abbey said, "Do not think on Sir. That is just his way. Sir must have the final say of everything." Maybe now, I think, but maybe not always, if I could ever get my freedom.

Monday, July 17, 1854
Alexandria, Virginia

I could scarcely breathe for holding Abbey so tight. How can I leave Abbey and the only home I know? My arms have never reached around her waist. But we both have a surprise now. My arms wrap all the way round her shoulders. "You are a growing child," Abbey said, and laughed. "Soon you will be a fine-sounding grown lady." Then she put something in my hand. It was a piece of blue satin cloth. "Jane Mae was saving this swatch for your story panel. She said that pretty blue must be the color of a freedom-blue sky." I love Abbey, and I know she loves me.

Tuesday, July 18 1854
Baltimore, Mary's Land

We left early in the morning, before the sunrise. After Sir saw to the trunks being loaded onto the carriage, he drove off in his wagon. Mistress did not say a word to him and he did not watch to see her go. I thought he would accompany us on the trip. It is not proper for Mistress to go alone. But he sent along an overseer, Mr. Thomas Hatchett, to accompany us the whole way. Abbey warned me, "Watch and stay close to Mistress and far from Mr. Thomas Hatchett. He is a hate-filled man."

Mr. Hatchett took us in the carriage to Washington, DC. I was tired enough to sleep the whole way there, but I did not sleep. As Mistress slept, I looked out the window and thought of my mother and when she would take me for walks in the woods. *The sun rises in the east, Eliza, and goes back down in the west.* And I wondered, *From where is she seeing this sun rise today?* It is a hard thought that Mama does not know about this journey I am taking with the mistress.

We arrived at the station just in time for boarding. There was so much noise and commotion. A steam train is a most loud and powerful thing. It whistles. It spouts steam and blows smoke everywhere. The sound of the train is so loud. I had to cover my ears. We took the steam train to Baltimore, Mary's Land.

Immediately Mistress and I were loaded into a cabin car. I am allowed to sit with Mistress in the Ladies' Car. It is much nicer than any other car and is farthest away from the heat, noise, and smell of the engine. Mr. Hatchett may sit with Mistress here also, but thankfully he preferred to sit with the menfolk in the Smoker Car. Normally, I would not ride with Mistress, but I was grateful that she demanded that I stay at her side. Mr. Hatchett saw to the baggage being loaded. The train conductor's voice shouted, "All aboard," many, many times before bells clanged and clanged louder and louder. Then the whistle screamed, *Whoo. WHOO. WHOOO.* It is so loud I must cover my ears again.

The train started to move with a jolt. All my insides shook and trembled at the sound of it. Slowly at first, and then it jerked and pulled. It puffed along like it could not catch its breath. But steadily and slowly, it breathed and puffed harder and faster, gaining and picking up speed. In no time we were steaming along down the tracks. This train car is most fine with very fine ladies here. But something went wrong with the track and we had to wait for it to be fixed. It was a very hot day.

When we arrived in Baltimore, the first thing I learned was that we had to stay overnight in a hotel, as we missed the steamboat to Cambridge. There would not be another one until first thing in the morning. Mistress was calm all the while. I have never seen her like this before. I kept close to her so she would not have to worry about me. The hotel is so fine and beautiful. Here even the Slaves working in the hotel are dressed very fine and better than Sir! I wish I could tell Abbey everything I see.

Wednesday, July 19, 1854
Eastern Shores of Mary's Land, Dorchester County

The steamboat was just as loud as the train, though I loved the paddling sound of the boat and lapping sound of the water. I was glad to spend the entire journey at my mistress's side in her cabin. Though she was not ailing like before, she did not want to walk on the deck of the boat. She was sick and tired of the Chesapeake Bay and Choptank River waters moving the boat side to side and up and down. She moaned for the whole journey. She could keep nothing in her stomach. I read to her to calm her.

Mistress complained that the boat was slow. It took five hours to arrive, but it seemed fast to me. Mr. Edward, Mistress's brother-in-law, came to fetch us in their fine brougham coach. He looked to be a kind man. He helped Mistress into the carriage and then me. He told Mr. Hatchett to load the trunks. I did not have to help load Mistress's heavy trunks. And finally, Mr. Hatchett accompanied us no more. Thankfully, I never encountered Thomas Hatchett or his temper.

Thursday, July 20, 1854
Eastern Shores of Mary's Land, Dorchester County

Upon our arrival to the home of Mistress Susan, I learned my mistress is a twin! In appearance, my mistress and her sister are as identical as identical can be. Yet they seem as different as the night is from the day. Looking at them side by side, it is clear Mistress is very sick. But even in her low state she brightens up happy in the sight of her kin. They were so happy to see each other. Still, I cannot help the sorry feeling I have for her. I found out my mistress's name. It is Mistress Margaret. I never knew this before.

Life with Doe in Mary's Land

July 21, 1854–March 2, 1855

Friday, July 21, 1854
Eastern Shores of Mary's Land, Dorchester County

I am someplace so far away from everything I know. This is Mary's Land. But I declare, some places have the prettiest names. It is a most pretty place as I have ever seen. I have seen more of Mary's Land than my own home state of Virginia.

Saturday, July 22, 1854
Eastern Shores of Mary's Land, Dorchester County

There are so many new things. Some things are the same. First, there is Doe. She is the same in station as Abbey back home. She is the cook and in charge of the kitchen and what happens in the house. She has a daughter Nellie. I wanted to tell Doe I can carry water but I remembered dropping Abbey's soup pot. Maybe my hands are not as strong as they once were. Sarah does the laundry in the house, but she does not live in the Big House with the other house Slaves. She lives in the quarters with her father. He is called Old Joe.

Sir raised mostly tobacco. Here on Mr. Edward's farm they raise corn, pumpkins, barley, wheat, and so many things Sir does not raise. Also, Mr. Edward is what is called a water man. His family has farmed the waters of the Chesapeake Bay. They take oysters, crabs, turtles, and fish from these waters.

This day Doe took a long look at me. Mistress Susan did the same. Finally Mistress Susan said, "You are sure enough Jane Mae's child."

"You knew my mother?" I asked Doe.

"Yes," she said. "She served Mistress Margaret since we were girls." That made me happy that I am known in the world so far away from my mother, Abbey, and my home.

But then Doe said, "I cannot believe your master would do such a thing to your poor mama and to your poor Mistress Susan." And that took all my happy feelings away.

Sunday, July 23, 1854
Eastern Shores of Mary's Land, Dorchester County

The second day I was here I was so grateful to Doe. She gave me a homespun dress and apron with two pockets to replace my itchy sack dress. This dress is soft cotton with nice deep side pockets. Sir never let us wear clothes with pockets. He said having pockets puts the temptation of stealing into a Slave's mind.

I am very glad to be so far away from Sir.

Monday, July 24, 1854
Eastern Shores of Mary's Land, Dorchester County

Today Doe gave me hard-soled, high-button shoes; they pinched my toes at first because I did not have them on the right feet. When I got them straightened out, they felt fine and clicked on the floor when I walked. It's a softer click than Sir's big heavy boots. But Mistress told me if she hears me click them once she will take them away.

Wednesday, July 26, 1854
Eastern Shores of Mary's Land, Dorchester County

No sooner did I wear my new shoes than Mistress took them from me. She had me put them under the foot of her bed to stay. But when I went to my sleeping pallet, I saw them and I took them back. I hid them in my pallet. I wish Abbey were here so that I may ask her if taking something back that belongs to you is like stealing. I pray not.

Thursday, July 27, 1854
Eastern Shores of Mary's Land, Dorchester County

Today Doe gave me soft-soled shoes made of deerskin leather. They are called moccasins. I have never seen the likes of them. They are beautiful and fit my feet perfectly. And best of all, they do not make noise when I walk. Now I do not worry about Mistress hearing me. I returned my hard-soled shoes back to under her bed.

Saturday, August 5, 1854
Eastern Shores of Mary's Land, Dorchester County

Mistress Susan wants to do everything for my mistress. But still I can hardly find the time to write. She sent me to see Doe for chores in the kitchen. But every day I go to Doe, she says she doesn't know what she can do with me.

Today Doe sent me to the storage room closet behind the room where my mistress and I sleep to fetch a pile of clothes stored there. Underneath the clothes was a stack of newspapers tied together. What I found in the pages I could not believe, but with my own eyes, I read them.

The newspapers did not contain news of the day as I read back home to Mistress in Alexandria, Virginia. This newspaper, called the *New Era Newspaper,* contained short stories, poems, and letters written by everyday persons. These stories were from our country and abroad. And most of what was written on the pages was about ending Slavery. There was one story in particular that was printed in chapter parts over the weeks' editions called *Uncle Tom's Cabin.* The whole book was there. While Mistress rested, I read in secret through chapter two because I could not put it down. These chapters tell of the place called Kentucky where Jane Mae is now, I think. The woman is named Eliza. Her husband, George, was taken away from his factory work and toiled under a cruel owner. They had one surviving child, a son, Harry.

Thursday, August 17, 1854
Eastern Shores of Mary's Land, Dorchester County

Today when I went to see Doe, I asked her permission to make the all-heal remedy for my mistress. I told her I am to give the remedy to Mistress all year-round now. But Doe said she would do it if I tell her how. She is just like Abbey in this way. She is most particular about her kitchen area. Today I read another chapter of the book in the newspaper. George is running away to Canada with the hopes that he can buy freedom for his wife and their child. I pray this story comes out well in the end. I pray for all three.

Sunday, August 20, 1854
Eastern Shores of Mary's Land, Dorchester County

Today Doe's little boy, Peyton, came to the kitchen. He is eight years old. He is not so big as yet, but he had a big chore. And he is Doe's pride. Mr. Edward had him pick up the chicken feathers in the chicken yard. I asked if I could help. But he does not seem to be too sure about me. He studied me carefully before Doe said, "Yes."

But when we got to the yard there was a huge ruckus. A fox was in the chicken house. Peyton began to whoop and holler. I grabbed a stick and the washtub from the yard. I went to the other side of the chicken coop, banging the washtub. Poor little Peyton came face-to-face with that bushy-tailed fox. I declare Peyton was as scared as that bushy-tailed rascal. Everybody came running out to the yard to see what the fuss was all about.

The fox got none of Mr. Edward's hens. But the chicken yard was a mess of feathers. And that was even more work. Peyton and I were collecting feathers nearly the whole day.

"Feathers will come in handy for Mistress and Master's pillows and bedding," Peyton said, already sounding like his big self. And that day Peyton and I became best friends.

Tuesday, August 22, 1854
Eastern Shores of Mary's Land, Dorchester County

The sun was very hot today. I asked Sarah where I could hang my quilt to air it out. She told me to hang it on the clothesline. When I hung it on there, it caused a great commotion. Peyton saw the picture panel of the bushy-tailed fox and he went running and calling for Doe to come look.

He came back, pulling Doe with him. Then Doe, Sarah, and Peyton came to look. "This is my story quilt," I said. And I told them how my mother had stitched my favorite stories in it. Peyton pointed to the picture of the fox. I was afraid this brought up his fear again.

"A fox is not a thing to fear," I said. "One time a rooster outsmarted a fox, right in his own barnyard." And before I knew it, I was remembering the story right from my quilt. This is how I told the story to them:

A rooster ruled over everything in his yard. As soon as the sun began to rise, he crowed perfect and loud. He was a proud thing but too careless for his own good. One morning, a fox came into the barnyard. Be careful, *his friends and family told Rooster. To show he wasn't afraid, he was going to walk right past the fox.*

"Where you going?" say Fox. "They tell me you have the voice of an angel. Please, friend, let me hear you sing."

Rooster did not have to be asked twice. He stood up high on his toes, closed his eyes, and planned to sing a most beautiful song. Just as he started, that fox showed what he was. Before you knew anything, Fox grabbed Rooster in his teeth and started carrying him away to his home in the woods.

Fear rose up in Rooster's chest but he knew he had to do something to save his own life. I should be careful, *he told himself,* but do not fear. *"Sir," he said to the fox, "take pity on me. Give me time to say good-bye to my family." Fox was going to answer yes.*

But the moment that sly rascal opened his mouth to reply, Rooster flew to the highest branch of an acorn tree and out of reach of that fox and his teeth! "Come back down," pleaded Fox. "Poor Rooster," Fox begged. "I didn't mean to frighten you. If you will just come down, I will tell you what I really wanted, and it has nothing to do with my stomach."

"Oh no, no, no!" Rooster say from high above. "I am free from you now. I won't be fooled again."

"Yes," Doe said to me. "You certainly are Jane Mae's daughter."

Wednesday, August 23, 1854
Eastern Shores of Mary's Land, Dorchester County

Thankfully this day was quiet, but something wouldn't let me rest. Then I saw the calendar page and I knew why. Today, back home in Alexandria is the Slave auction day that Sir was aiming to get ready for. I pray Sir did not go to the Slave auction. I pray he did not sell me or Abbey away. While Mistress slept, I read more of the book from the *New Era Newspaper.* But the story is most sad and nothing good happens for the poor Slave and it shows how bad Slavery is. In this chapter there is Uncle Tom and Aunt Chloe's cabin. There is a prayer meeting at the cabin and they sing, "O Canaan, bright Canaan, I'm bound for the land of Canaan," while poor Tom, without even knowing it, has been sold away to a trader.

This story is most sad, but I must find a way to read more. Reading of these poor souls—George,

Eliza, and Harry, Uncle Tom and Aunt Chloe—I do not know what is the worse thing: to live the life of the Slave, or to live it and read how bad it is for others as well.

Saturday, August 26, 1854
Eastern Shores of Mary's Land, Dorchester County

Last night while I watched over my mistress rest, I heard singing and talking from down in the woods. The next day I asked Doe about it. "It was Meeting Day," she said. I cannot tell anyone this but it is just the same as it is in *Uncle Tom's Cabin*. Here Slaves are allowed to meet once in a month. They sing songs or play drums and listen to Old Joe talk the Bible. Back home, Sir never let us have a praise house or a meeting day.

Doe and Sarah said I should come to the next one. Next month it will be the last Friday if they are not shucking corn. That will be 29 September. But Doe said if it is corn shucking time, Meeting Day will not happen until the next month. When it is corn shucking time, that is all that can be done.

But Sarah said if it is a meeting day, I must come. I know I am probably disallowed. But I will ask my mistress.

Friday, September 1, 1854
Eastern Shores of Mary's Land, Dorchester County

Today I met Old Joe. I think he is wise like my Abbey back home. Here all the field workers live close to the crops in cabins they call the quarters. There are fourteen cabins in two rows, which makes a street walkway down the middle. Old Joe lives in the first log cabin at the beginning of their quarter. He lives with Sarah, his daughter, and her son, Snowden. Old Joe's cabin is called the praise house. But sometimes, he said, they praise in the woods behind the quarters.

Wednesday, September 6, 1854
Eastern Shores of Mary's Land, Dorchester County

I want to go to Meeting Day if we are not shucking corn then.

Monday, September 18, 1854
Eastern Shores of Mary's Land, Dorchester County

Meeting Day has stopped. Tandy, Mr. Edward's top hand, says when it is time to harvest the corn. Corn shucking takes more than two hands and more than they have on this farm. Mr. Edward sent for help from Bailey Farm, the next farm over. There is so much work to be done before the rains get to the corn. Above all else the corn must stay dry.

Thursday, September 21, 1854
Eastern Shores of Mary's Land, Dorchester County

Mistress Susan and Mistress Margaret will help, too. Sometimes they laugh and giggle like Doe said they did when they were girls. I wonder if my mistress was like that with Mama.

Monday, September 25, 1854
Eastern Shores of Mary's Land, Dorchester County

Today everyone was shucking corn. First the corn was brought in from the field. It was stacked in the crib to stay dry. Next we took off the husks. The husks needed to be kept clean and dry. The shucks will be saved for Slave and animal bedding.

Some corn will be used for animal feed. Some corn is kept on the cob for seed corn to be planted. Doe said all of this must be done by November. By then the rest of the corn is to be ground to make meal. Doe said I may have some of the husks to make a doll. This will keep hands busy during the winter while we wait for spring.

Tandy said after planting the corn to count 180 days for the harvest. That is six calendar pages and then some, depending on the growing season. Mr. Edward said he plans to give the Bailey hands a fair share for their farm for their help. Then he will sell some, but mostly he will use it. Doe says the first chance she gets she will make succotash; it is made with corn and beans and other vegetables. She says it is very tasty. Abbey probably would not mind corn shucking over doing tobacco. Everyone helps and there is no bad tobacco smell.

Saturday, September 30, 1854
Eastern Shores of Mary's Land, Dorchester County

Mistress has a happier look here than home in Virginia. She is very talky with Mistress Susan and Mr. Edward. Once she asked me, how do I get along with the other Slaves? I told her the truth, how they are most kind to me. Mistress Margaret is still sickly but her spirit soars high with her family. It makes me ache for my mother once more.

Saturday, October 7, 1854
Eastern Shores of Mary's Land, Dorchester County

This night I had a dream. It was about my mother and Abbey. First I am standing next to Mama. Then she is gone. Next I stand close to Abbey. Then she is gone. Then I am standing alone. When I woke up, I felt I would never see Mama or Abbey again. The bright moonlight woke me so I read from the newspaper book. It is a hard story. Poor Tom was promised his freedom by his master, Mr. Shelby, but now he shall not have it. This trader, Mr. Haley, is a harsh man; he forced Shelby to sell Eliza's little baby, Harry, because of debts he owes. But thankfully Eliza escapes with her baby in her arms. Now it is hard to sleep with so much fear for Eliza and poor little Harry.

Tuesday, October 10, 1854
Eastern Shores of Mary's Land, Dorchester County

We hardly finished the corn and now it is time to bring in the hard-rind pumpkins. We must stack them for to use later. At the same time, apples must be harvested. Old Joe knows which apples are best for pulping and juicing for applejack. He said it is a good,

good apple season. Mistress Susan was glad to know that. Then she talked with Doe about which apples to use for drying.

Monday, October 16, 1854
Eastern Shores of Mary's Land, Dorchester County

This morning while I was buttoning Mistress's dress she could hardly catch her breath. Now she has started a cough. Mistress Susan sent for the doctor. Doe knew where the all-heal herb grows in abundance. Doe helped me gather it. While we walked, Doe asked me if I would attend Meeting Day. The time is not right to ask my mistress yet. I have a few days left.

Thursday, October 19, 1854
Eastern Shores of Mary's Land, Dorchester County

Finally Doe let me help her in the kitchen. She had me make the food packets that she leaves out for Old Joe and some of the other Slaves who work in the field. I took day-old bread and leftover meat, usually bacon, and tied it in the food cloths.

Tuesday, October 24, 1854
Eastern Shores of Mary's Land, Dorchester, County

This evening, before I could even speak of it, Mistress said, "Eliza, you must not attend Meeting Day. Your master would disallow it and I may have need of you." And for the first time I was surprised by the anger that burned in my throat. I wished to scream from my mouth but Abbey's words came to me, "Never let Mistress see this Eliza." I swallowed it all and slept fitfully for a while.

Saturday, October 28, 1854
Eastern Shores of Mary's Land, Dorchester County

Last night, Meeting Day, the house was most quiet. Mistress Susan and Mr. Edward left for a visit to Bailey Farm. My mistress went to bed early and was already in the deep part of sleep. From my pallet and all through the night, I heard the voices of Doe, Sarah, Nellie, and the others singing and shouting. *How I wish I could be there,* I repeated as I hugged my quilt and dreamed of it. But right before dawn, I woke up. I heard more singing. It was not a dream. It was not the song in the wind. I thought it might be Sarah or Doe. But it was not their voices. It was someone else. My mistress was still in the deepest part of sleep. I got up from my pallet and ran to the woods. Behind the house, beyond the rise and over the hill, there is a path between the rows of red maple trees. I entered it where the ground is padded with weeds and moist soil. The morning air was cold and the scent was sweet. I heard something behind me. I turned to see a woman. I did not recognize her from the other Slaves here on Mr. Edward's farm. She stood before me, nodding her head in greeting, and I did the same. I thought, *How small she looks standing next to the big tree.* "My name is Eliza," I told her. "Harriet is my name," she replied. She said nothing more, but her strong presence commanded me to listen. And she started to sing the song again. She continued to sing her song to me. The words were most clear. When her song ended, she vanished into the woods as fast as she had come.

At rising time, while I was combing Mistress's hair, I asked if she had heard the singing, too. "No, Eliza," she said, coughing. But the rest of the house was all in whisper. When I went to the kitchen for the all-heal, Doe and Sarah and now Nellie were already there.

This morning everyone was talking about the good time they had had. Sarah told me about the Shout.

She said everybody sings the words of the song as loud as they can. They dance and shout out the songs for the glory of the good and loving Almighty God. I told her that is what I had heard. But then I told them that was not all I heard. And I told them about the woman I saw and the song she sang to me. This is as I remember the words:

When that old chariot comes,
I'm gonna lead you.
I'm bound for the Promised Land.
I'm gonna lead you,
On freedom road.

Doe and Sarah and Nellie knew who this woman was. And they knew the song she sang.

"That was Moses," Nellie told me. "We call her the Moses of our people."

"But she called herself Harriet," I said.

"That is right. She is called Minty, too. Miss Harriet Tubman came last night," Doe said. "She ran away to her freedom. Patrollers tried but she never ever got caught. Now she comes back to show others the way to freedom! For those that follow her, she tells them you cannot look behind. You only look in front."

Sarah added, "That is right. That was Miss Harriet walking along the road singing to the people—telling them to get ready. Lord, she sing the farewell message. It say, 'Be ready in spring.'"

I looked from Nellie to Doe and to Sarah. My head was spinning. I have heard Sir speak of this woman. I have read newspaper accounts about this woman. This is the very woman Sir wanted to have captured! Now my prayer will be that Sir should never catch her in his bare hands. And I thought, *I have talked to this woman; I have seen her with my very eyes.*

"Moses said, *Let my people go!*" Doe chimed in.

"Yes," I said. And before I could stop myself, I told them the story from my story quilt as I remember it from the Good Book. I am writing it here too so it will always be close to my heart:

> *Moses led his people out of bondage from Israel. Pharaoh ruled harshly over the Hebrew people and he was harsh. He decreed, "Every boy baby of the Hebrew race must die." Moses' mother hid him for three months and all the while she prayed to the Living and Almighty God, "Take care of my baby." She made a cradle for him and took him down to the river and hid him among the reeds.*
>
> *One day, Pharaoh's daughter came to the riverside. She saw the beautiful child and she took him home. She named him Moses and raised him like her own. Moses grew into a great man among the*

Egyptians. Moses knew he was Hebrew. He saw how Pharaoh mistreated his people. He didn't know how to help but he knew he had to. He left Egypt and went to the desert. He became a shepherd for a man named Jethro. Moses took to carrying a shepherd's stick. He married Jethro's daughter.

All this time, Moses prayed to God to show him how to help his people. All the while, he grew in strength and his wisdom. Now Moses could use power-compelling speech to talk to God! After a time, God spoke to Moses out of a burning bush. You must make my people free from Pharaoh. *Moses didn't know how. Then God said,* Do not worry about that. That worry is mine. Study on me and do what I tell you. Go see Pharaoh.

Moses was obedient. He stood before Pharaoh. He stretched out his walking stick. God turned it into a slithery snake. God showed Pharaoh sign after sign. God commanded Pharaoh: Let my people go! *Pharaoh wasn't even studying about God.*

But God sent worse and sore troubles to the people of Israel. Finally Pharaoh was frightened. He let the Israelites go but he did not keep his word. He sent his armies after them. When the Israelites got to the Red Sea, they did not know how to get across the raging waters. Pharaoh's army was steady gaining on them. Then God spoke to Moses: Stretch out *your staff over the seas. And the most wondrous thing happened. The waters parted and the children of Israel walked out of Egypt into the Promised Land. Pharaoh's army tried to follow. But God would not hold back the wall of water.*

When the children of Israel saw that God had made them safe, they sang a beautiful song before they were on their way again.

"Just like Moses in the Bible led his people, our Moses will lead us," Nellie said.

"Anybody want to go to freedom can follow her. Miss Harriet will be back," Doe said. "Just be ready come the spring. Old Joe knows."

Sunday, November 5, 1854
Eastern Shores of Mary's Land, Dorchester County

The weather is turning cold. Mistress's health is turning worse. Mistress Susan and I stay close to her while everyone else is getting ready for slaughtering and butchering. First they will slaughter cows. After Christmas season is over, in January, they will slaughter and butcher the hogs. Then Doe will be busy rendering lard and salting pork for the smokehouse. Later this morning Mistress Susan sent me to help bring firewood to stack. I was glad to be far from Mistress's sick room.

Saturday, November 11, 1854
Eastern Shores of Mary's Land, Dorchester County

Today Mistress slept for a long time. She hardly wants to rise to eat. I fed her clear soup. Mistress Susan sent me to the kitchen to help Doe. But then Doe said tomorrow I must go to bring food to Old Joe and all-heal to Sarah. Now Sarah is down with a cold. I wish I could return to the newspaper book, but there is so much to do. I want to know what has happened to Eliza. Is she safe now?

Sunday, November 12, 1854
Eastern Shores of Mary's Land, Dorchester County

While I visited with Old Joe I told him about the woman I met in the woods and her song and how it sings around inside me like a circle. I told him how I tried to bury it away inside my mind but cannot stop hearing it. Then we sang her song for a while. Maybe I told him too many things. I told him about the newspaper stories I read to my mistress in Virginia. I told him about wanting tickets on the underground railroad train. I told him one day I want to be bound to the Land of Promise. But when? Old Joe laughed. "The underground railroad is more than a train," he told me. And I wanted to know more. He told me there are station houses and "friends" who help. He told me there is a station house some thirty or more miles north and east of here. He said getting to that safe house is my ticket on the underground railroad.

Then I told Old Joe of Abbey and Sir back home in Virginia. But Old Joe knew my mother and Mistress when they were girls. Mistress's name is Margaret Bailey. My mother, Jane Mae, was a Slave from the next farm over, Bailey Farm. Old Joe knew about my mother and her stories, too. I told him of my story quilt. And I told him the secret gift Mistress gave to me—the ability to read and write. And I showed him. I took my writing book from my pocket. I told him about the newspaper book I found in the storage closet of Mistress's room. Then Old Joe opened up the Bible and handed me some papers to read to him. They are his manumission papers, his freedom papers. Old Joe is a free man. He does no work. He only tends to his garden and goes fishing now. He lives in the quarters. He said, "This is the only place I know how to live. I can go no where else." Mr. Edward's father gave him the Bible and his freedom papers in it like he said he would when he died. I know Sir would never give Abbey or me our freedom. I told Old Joe my biggest worry and fear: my mistress is surely sick, maybe too sick to return home, with me. And, when I return home, without my mistress to protect me, Sir will probably say my high time done come and sell me as he has done to my mother. Old Joe didn't say another thing to this. He wanted to talk about the words of the Good Book.

Old Joe knows the Bible but cannot read the words. So I played a book game with him that Mistress played with me when she taught me my gift. He was to say a name for a book in the Bible, and then I find it so he can see what the words look like. He thought a while. He said, "Genesis."

"That one is easy to find," I said. That is the first book. I showed him the page and the words. He ran his hand over the page in the book. He said the word "Genesis" like it was for the first time.

Then he wanted to see what the words "Promised Land" look like. That took a little longer for me to find. I showed him those words. He said them. Then Old Joe was quiet a long time. We just sat and did not talk. Then he said, "Eliza, I think you interested in getting your freedom, but no one will give you that. You will have to take it. I cannot tell you to go or not to go. It is a dangerous road. You still barely a child. Patrollers with Slave-catching dogs are sometimes more frightful than the worst master." Then he started humming the circle tune. Finally he said to me, "Eliza, you can read and write."

"Yes," I said.

"Then that makes you bigger than even the man who tries to keep you a Slave."

When it was time to leave, Old Joe said to come again. He said, "I certainly enjoyed your company." No one ever said that to me before.

Thursday, November 23, 1854
Eastern Shores of Mary's Land, Dorchester County

Everyone is filling up with happiness and light. Everything is busy, busy now. Christmas preparation starts early here. It is a month away and we are all getting ready for a Christmas celebration. For Christmas season, Slaves are allowed to see their families on other farms. Some people will go to the city of Baltimore. Doe says Mr. Edward lets them go because he knows they will come back when it is time.

Tuesday, December 12, 1854
Eastern Shores of Mary's Land, Dorchester County

So many people come every day. They are arriving for the Christmas celebration week. Some others leave to visit their kin on nearby plantations. Only the house Slaves are not allowed to visit anyone. In the house the work never stops. But still, everyone feels the joy and lightness of the holiday time.

Tuesday, December 19, 1854
Eastern Shores of Mary's Land, Dorchester County

Mistress slept all the day long today. Mistress Susan said that is good, but I know she is as worried as I am.

Monday, December 25, 1854
Eastern Shores of Mary's Land, Dorchester County

It is Christmas Day. Mistress felt well enough to sit by the fire in the sitting room. In front of everyone she showed me a great kindness. She gave me two presents and the kindest words I have ever heard. The first is a ready-made shawl. The second is an apron that she made when she was a girl. "Keep it clean, Eliza, like your thoughts and deeds," she told me.

Then I said, "I have something for you, too, Mistress." And I handed her the corn-husk doll I had made. Inside the shucks I stuffed it with the all-heal. "I hope it can make you feel better," I told her.

Mistress said, "Thank you, Eliza," And I felt she meant it.

Doe said Mistress is kind to know how hard I try to remedy her ailments. But this is not the only thing. I remember what Abbey told me long ago about how Slaves have to be two of them selves. I wonder if this is true for Mistress, too. She is not the same mistress as the one in Virginia.

Monday, January 1, 1855
Eastern Shores of Mary's Land, Dorchester County

Happy new year! Everyone here in this house, Slave and master, salute each and one and the other with a cheerful greeting: "I wish you a happy new year!" And then the other receiving the greeting says, "I wish you the same."

Monday, January 8, 1855
Eastern Shores of Mary's Land, Dorchester County

The cold, wet weather prohibits any outside farming. Inside work takes the place of farming labor. Metal tools are sharpened, wooden handles are replaced or fixed, and leather straps are mended. I hardly see Doe. She is tending and preparing the hogs for slaughter and the meat to be cured in the smokehouse. Sarah says this is the quiet time while we wait for the signs of spring.

Thursday, January 11, 1855
Eastern Shores of Mary's Land, Dorchester County

Today Mistress is very low. Mistress Susan and I worry at her bedside together. I told her what Abbey said, that Mistress is always worse in the winter months. But I fear she is weaker now than last winter. I will keep giving Mistress the all-heal until the doctor can come again. I will do everything I can to help her get well. But winter is just starting up. Her cough is growing very, very bad.

I wish Abbey were here. She would know what to do.

Thursday, January 18, 1855
Eastern Shores of Mary's Land, Dorchester County

I am worried, worried for my mistress. But I am also so worried for me.

Friday, February 2, 1855
Eastern Shores of Mary's Land, Dorchester County

Early this morning Old Joe was in the kitchen with Doe. He said something to me he has already said before: "When the mind is made up, the road becomes clear." This night while Mistress was deep in sleep, I rose. Outside, the full moon glows bright but the North Star shines even brighter. Could it be calling me to come home? But where is home for me now? It is not Virginia. That I know.

Saturday, February 17, 1855
Eastern Shores of Mary's Land, Dorchester County

The doctor came today to see Mistress Margaret. But he did not bleed her. She was too weak. She wheezes, hardly able to breathe. I boiled lemon and mint leaves to make steam so Mistress could take in the vapors. I do not know if this will help.

Friday, March 2, 1855
Eastern Shores of Mary's Land, Dorchester County

Old Joe was in the kitchen with Sarah and Doe humming my little song. He stopped humming to speak to me. "Eliza," he said, "something new always comes in with the wind. It's coming soon." And he went back to humming my little song.

Whispers in the Wind

March 23–May 18, 1855

Friday, March 23, 1855
Eastern Shores of Mary's Land, Dorchester County

Today there was a pretty tune on the wind. Yesterday Doe tied bottles to the tree in the kitchen yard. Everyone says when the bottle tree sings, that is a good sign. Warm weather will come soon. I pray it will help Mistress.

Tuesday, April 10, 1855
Eastern Shores of Mary's Land, Dorchester County

This is the first chance to write. My birthday has come and gone. I am thirteen now. I did not know it until Peyton ran from the river bringing rocks to show. Looking at his rock pile I remembered this is the first time I did not count the rocks in Abbey's rock jar. Last night I cried and cried for missing everything I once had: the only life I ever knew and Abbey and my mother, Jane Mae. I am thirteen. Sarah clicked her tongue and said it is a bad-luck number. But Doe said I have that already. Now she said maybe my luck will happen in reverse.

Thursday, April 12, 1855
Eastern Shores of Mary's Land, Dorchester County

Troubles come and more troubles. All day it rained. Abbey says some rain is good; too much rain brings trouble. But there was more than a little trouble here. Mistress coughs blood. It was a sad day.

Monday, April 16, 1855
Eastern Shores of Mary's Land, Dorchester County

Trouble has come! Dr. Nable finally came to see about Mistress. I hate to think to say it, but it might be too late now. She is real, real bad now. The bleeding cures he can give won't help at all. He uses Mary's Land eastern shores leeches, not the precious little leeches from France as Dr. Hardy did. Still, it makes her worse off. I wish he had something else to try.

Monday, May 7, 1855
Eastern Shores of Mary's Land, Dorchester County

This is the worst of news. Today a letter arrived from Sir. It's very hard to read. Sir's writing hand is terrible and he spells very poorly. I did my best to read it to Mistress but she was too weak to hear what it says. The letter reads that Sir is finally coming here in four weeks to see about Mistress. He says he is going to fetch us home! This letter was written seven days ago. That means Sir will be here in three weeks' time. My insides turned weak like reeds in the wind. My legs did not hold me. Everything inside of me was like an earthquake. I lay down on my pallet. I wrapped in my quilt. I kept telling myself I cannot go back with Sir. I closed my eyes and heard the little song inside of me. And I decided: I will not go back with Sir. I will do as the wind tells me. I will go home. But I will go north to freedom.

Thursday, May 17, 1855
Eastern Shores of Mary's Land, Dorchester County

Nothing inside of me was quiet. Listening to Mistress, her breath so rough and dry, I wondered if she would last the rough ride home for four days.

It was the deep part of night when I rose from my bed. I walked from the house toward the quarters. Old Joe was sitting on his porch like he was waiting for my visit. Now I am certain of what I must do.

Friday, May 18, 1855
Eastern Shores of Mary's Land, Dorchester County

I am sitting quietly now as I write. This morning I took my shoes back from under Mistress Margaret's bed and I put them in my bundle. Once, I had been afraid Mistress would take them from me, but this does not frighten me anymore. I would not leave my shoes behind. But I did not wear them. Someone would hear the heels click. It would have taken too much time to lace them. I watched Mistress Margaret's shallow breathing for a long while. There was nothing I could do for her, now. I said good-bye but she does not know this. I went to the kitchen house. I filled food packets heavy with thick bacon and corn bread. I stuffed one into the pocket of my apron. I put another and another and another into my bundle, four altogether. I took the filled water pouch, too, and my story quilt. I ran down the path into the dark murky night, through the gate. The ground was cold. I left my moccasins behind. A voice inside me said: *Do not look behind you tonight, Eliza.* There were no bright stars to flicker and twinkle. There was no moon, only heavy gray clouds. The smell of rain was in the air. There was no story wind inside me this night, just one word.

Run! I ran, ran, ran to the trees. "Keep running," Old Joe had said, "until you see the daylight come again. Then you can rest." I kept his voice in my mind, running all the while.

Escape

May 19–May 26. 1855

Saturday, May 19, 1855
Eastern Shores of Mary's Land, Dorchester County

I have escaped and I can hardly catch my breath. I cannot think of what I have done. I can only think of Eliza and Harry from the book.

At night I moved deeper and deeper into the forest. Hardly my first and second steps made me remember Old Joe's warning about the sweet gum trees. The seedpod is a spiny, prickly burr and was everywhere I stepped. I had to stop and pull the burrs from both my feet. I wanted to cry out in pain, but it was too late for that. I put on my shoes, but the damage was already done. Old Joe said I must travel north and east to get to the safe house. Soon I would come to a square-shaped rock that is as big as I am.

The night I visited Old Joe, he told me about three signs to watch for to let me know I was traveling in the right direction. I prayed I would find them. His words fill my head: "Don't ever look back, walk east, and stay along the line of the trees to the river. Travel the night. Sleep the day. Follow the line of trees along the stream. Go east. Keep your back to the setting of the sun. Travel that way seven days and nights. Come to the safe house with a candlelight in the window. Knock two times . . . two times more. Man named Tabbard—he know what next. That gal, Harriet, she'll take you. . . . Be ready to run.

"Sleep some, walk more," Old Joe had said.

Finally I saw the square-shaped rock and daylight on the rise. This was the time Old Joe had said to stop, eat, and rest. But thinking on what I have done will not let me rest. I have run away from my mistress. I will never see Abbey again. There will be no word of me to Mama unless I am caught. I can hear Sir say how he wants to catch me in his bare hands. I pray, pray, pray this will never happen. I wonder if I should have taken such a dangerous journey. Now I am alone.

In the thick of the trees, I found a hollowed-out place under a log where the ground was not so damp. Leaves and pine needles were stuck to mud on my shoes. I was too tired to clean them. The mud on my shoes is a heavy weight. I think of Mistress. If she is even breathing, I wonder, how many times has she called for Eliza? But she is all a dream, too. That life is my past; I cannot dwell on it. I must not think of Sir. I look around me. There is no one, just woods and trees and wind. This is all I have. The wind has stopped. My heart is quiet. I will sleep Sunday and at nightfall I will gather what little I have and move on.

Monday, May 21, 1855
Eastern Shores of Mary's Land, Dorchester County

Old Joe said it was best to leave Saturday to get a two-day head start on the patrollers, as they cannot gather a search party until Monday. I have been running for so long and I am afraid of getting caught. But at day when I stopped to rest, I forgot my fear for a while.

The sun was so bright. The sky was painted every blue I have ever seen. I thought of my satin cloth. White feathery clouds spread out in soft patches all around. Warblers and sparrows flitted and darted over me. My stomach grumbled and ached. But it was not food I wanted. It was only to be safe. I took a small piece of food, but my hunger was still deep. I ate the whole pack and drank most of the water. The sun warmed me and I slept but woke to every sound. I could not help but think: *What will prepare me for what comes next in the world?* There is no Mama or Abbey or Mistress to tell me what I must do to protect me now. There is no choice but to continue on.

Tuesday, May 22, 1855
Eastern Shores of Mary's Land, Dorchester County

I felt as though I was lost but I remembered my mother's words. *Eliza, you will never be lost.* This made me think of my story panel of the flying people. And I looked at another picture panel more closely—the compass. Mother had sewed that gadget onto the panel. Sure enough, I discovered that the little arrow on my compass pointing north showed me I am traveling the right way. And soon after, I found a second sign, three great trees that grew together, pointing like an arrow to the east. I know now I'm going the right way. But the cuts on my feet need care. All that I can do is use the food rags to wrap them.

The warm day turned itself over to a cool night. When I made my bundle for another night of walking I made sure I could see my compass before I moved on. I picked my way through the night of trees. The moon was not full but stars filled the black sky. Bullfrogs called in the tall grass. Rabbits passed me on the road. A deer family stood to watch me. I followed the sound in the wind. I followed the light of the moon. My head ran around in circles with the wind. *What have I done? Is Old Joe wrong? What if this house is not safe? Is Sir able to find me?*

The smell of rain came in quickly on the wind. I walked and walked in rain-soaked soil. I walked through marshy grass. I walked on wet, cold rocky ground. I always find time to write. My journal is my companion and friend.

Thursday, May 24, 1855
Eastern Shores of Mary's Land, Dorchester County

It is day. I have stopped to write and rest. But everything is very hard. My thoughts bring me so much sadness and make me afraid to shut my eyes. I am glad I can tell my little book. I always find time to write.

The rain finally stopped. One thing for sure, it will start again. As soon as night falls, I will start again as fast as I can in spite of my wounded feet. I have found a sturdy tree limb that bears some of my weight.

Friday, May 25, 1855
Eastern Shores of Mary's Land, Dorchester County

When I woke, I let myself be most cheery. I thought of my compass and how even though my mother is lost from me, she has given me what I need so I cannot get lost. And I remember her words as I write in my little book the story of how the people could fly to freedom. This is how I remember it:

> *There was once an old, old wood sawyer. He knew a great many things. Even then he was an old man, and he is so much older now, as this happened a long, long time ago. But he is gifted with a very good*

memory. And he will tell you he can remember a great many strange things that have happened in this world. He was there at the time when the Africans flew away with their women and children.

Once, all Africans could fly free like any bird. But when they came to these shores to slave in the fields, their pain and sadness was so great, they could not recall or remember how to take to the sky. Though some held on to their power of flight they looked like any other man and could not remember how to make it happen.

There was a most cruel master who worked the people hard in the cotton fields under the blazing sun. He hired the cruelest overseer, who drove the people hard, working men, women, and children from sunrise until long past sunset. He would not let them stop to rest during the midsummer sun. And all grew weak with heat and thirst. The overseer did not care if he worked them until they died.

There was a young woman among them new to this plantation, who had just borne her first child, and she had not completely regained her strength. She carried her baby with her to the field tied in swaddling cloth to her back. Being very weak, the woman stumbled, slipped, and fell. The baby cried. And the driver came running with his strap raised to strike. But the young woman stood, trying to continue chopping the knotgrass. She was very weak and sick from the heat. She stumbled and slipped and fell again. The young woman, in fear of her baby's life, spoke in the softest voice that soon became too loud for the overseer to hear. "Kuli-ba! Kuli-ba!" she said, as if they were words in a lullaby. She repeated the words again and again. Over and over she said the words, hoping the people around her could hear this message and remember. "Kuli-ba! Kuli-ba!" An old man in the field working next to her stopped. He mouthed the words. Then he repeated the words out loud, too. "Kuli-ba! Kuli-ba!" A young man in the field sang the words like a song. "Kuli-ba! Kuli-ba!" And then another woman and another man spoke the words. The people began to remember. They repeated the words over and over again. Soon the sound of those words had grown in the field as thick as knotgrass, as thick as cotton. And the people, one by one, stretched out their arms, leaped into the air, and were gone, like gulls or doves or crows, flying free over the fields and over the woods.

Thinking of this beautiful sight fills me with joy.

I fell asleep with the pencil in my hand. How long I was there I cannot say. I awoke to hear not-faraway voices. Something inside me said, *Hide.* I did, under a fallen sweet gum tree. There came two men on horses. They may have wanted to harm me. Horses' hooves kicked dirt on my face. Hiding here I prayed they would not find me. Their voices faded away. The beating of my heart rocked me into a restless sleep. And I slept more.

I was awakened a second time to feel something sticky running down my face. It was the sap of the sweet gum tree. I rose knowing I must keep going. My food and water are all but gone now; I drank what little rainwater I could catch in the pewter cup Doe gave me. It relieved some, but my thirst was great. I wondered how much longer until I found the safe house. The moonlight was a great help. I followed the stream as Old Joe said I must.

Saturday, May 26, 1855
Eastern Shores of Mary's Land, Dorchester County

Though the moon was growing in size, clouds were getting thick. It was a dark night. Through the forest from a distance I saw a pin light. Finally I could see another sign that I was going the right way, a third one—a small stream I had to ford. Then there was the smell of cook smoke. I was hardly able to walk but my will made me. Closer and closer I moved toward the little light. It was from a house tucked behind a small hill. I held on to my stick to steady myself and limped the rest of the way. As soon as I knocked—twice, and then twice more—the door opened. A man filled up the doorway. The yellow light of his lantern shone on his face. My head was hurting. My feet were hot and sticky. I was full of fear but the tired I felt was so much more. I could not believe I had traveled seven days.

"Can I help you?" the tall man said. His voice sounded most kind. I dropped to the ground. I knew I was falling. He reached for me and helped me to my feet.

"I . . . I . . . came a long way."

Someone else spoke through the open door. "Mr. Tabbard," the woman's voice said, "I knew she would be coming." I had heard that voice before. It was the woman, Harriet, I had met singing in the woods. It was the woman called Moses.

Even after I crossed the threshold of the safe house, Mr. Tabbard's door, the voice in the wind kept calling and singing to me:

When that old chariot comes,
I'm gonna lead you.
I'm bound for the Promised Land.
I'm gonna lead you,
On freedom road.

With the woman Harriet Tubman there, I knew that I was safe now.

The Safe House

May 29–June 1, 1855

Tuesday, May 29, 1855
Eastern Shores of Mary's Land, Dorchester County

I do not remember my first days here. I touch my chest where Abbey poked me so long ago and remember what I have done.

Old Joe called this the safe house. It is called a station house, too.

When I finally first took in my surroundings, the mistress of this house, Mrs. Tabbard, sat at the hearth sewing. She helped me to drink water. My thirst was so great. And she waited on me the way I have done for my mistress. From my pallet, I felt the warmth of the fire. I was given clean, dry clothes to wear. The mistress gave me clear soup. I tried to drink it slowly but could not. My hunger was as big as the room. Later, porridge was offered and I ate much more than usual. Normally it is not my favorite food, but it tasted good to me now. I noticed we were not alone in the good-size room. There was a fireplace, a table, stools, and sleeping places lined along three of the four walls. I counted six other runaway fugitives in this room. I lifted my head in greeting and to say thank you when I heard a child laugh. I saw two young boys who looked in age to be four or five and seven or eight.

On the far side of the room were four men and two women. Everyone stayed to their sleeping places except for the two young ones. First they stayed close to the wall. Then they crept across the wood floor, nearer to me or to the warmth of the fire. *Come close to me,* I thought. I did not know if they heard me. I was happy to be among friends, wrapped in my quilt.

"My name Silas," the big little one told me. "His name is David." He pointed to the other. "He is littler than me," he said. From that moment on, I called them Little One and Littler One.

The boys laughed and ran to the woman stoking the fire. They reminded me of myself when I was their age with my mother, Jane Mae.

"I am called Sally," the woman now tending the fire said. She touched the thick, heavy bandages on my feet. "Your cuts are not as bad as some others'," she said. "Your feet will be stronger for walking when they heal."

"Thank you," I managed to say.

First I am writing in my journal, but all I want to do is sleep more.

Wednesday, May 30, 1855
Eastern Shores of Mary's Land, Dorchester County

I slept the night through, and in the morning when I woke again, I felt stronger but my feet were tender. I scooted close to the fire to tend it. I put the ashes to the side to keep them hot for cooking the morning bread. I banked the logs. From the water bucket I filled the kettle and put it to heat.

"Someone taught you well," the mistress of this house said.

"I can fetch water, too," I said. "I am eager to help."

"Best you stay off your feet. Let them heal," she said. There was a pile of cloth that needed to be torn for bandages. I did this and noticed a pile of soiled bandages. I washed these in the bucket of water that was near the hearth while I sat close to the fire. Abbey always says to use hot vinegar, but this mistress said a soap bar is best. We are to wash our wounded feet with it, too.

Heavy clothes and blankets were gathered and handed out while mending was being done. The air will be warm during the day, but even in June to travel north, night can be a cold death. "Rest more," Mr. Tabbard told us. Our freedom journey would start on Saturday.

Thursday, May 31, 1855
Eastern Shores of Mary's Land, Dorchester County

Almost a whole week has passed since I ran. The rest and washing with the soap helped my cuts to heal quickly. My feet are tender but I hardly hurt or walk with a limp. The soft shoes this mistress gave me are bigger than my feet. "Better too big," Sally said. She showed me how to stuff them with rags for padding.

Today the smell of fresh-baked sweet bread filled up the room. The woman Harriet Tubman was among us. Mistress Tabbard does not call her by her given name. Here she is called Mistress Conductor or Conductor. She put her hands together and whispered prayers. We all did the same. Then she cut each one of us a piece of sweet bread as big as we wanted. Outside of Abbey's cooking, it was the most delicious thing I ever tasted.

With the bread we were given this night, Mistress Tabbard told us we were to have Meeting Night. There was no singing, shouting, or speaking the Bible the way Old Joe does. We spoke on anything that came to mind. It was very quiet at first. Then Mr. Adam Will spoke. "I had not been born into bondage, like my father. I was born a freedman. I am a merchant. I had been kidnapped not ten miles away from my own home in Rochester, New York, and forced into labor.

"I long to be rejoined with my family. It tears at me mightily," he said. And I admit I had never seen a grown man cry before.

Nancy was the cook for her master. "I have run

away with my son, Silas. My husband was killed. I could not let Silas suffer the way his father and I have. He must have a chance. We came from one of the Carolinas. I do not know which one. I had been traded back and forth so many times, it is hard to remember. But I remember that I was a little girl, smaller than Silas, when they carried me off in a sack from my family and my home. They put us on a ship and brought me here. I have run off so many times, I know my master will probably have me killed if I am taken back."

Squire said, "I am a blacksmith. I am very skilled in working with iron. My right name is Thomas Whitlock. People say because of my size, I fill up the room. I ran away because I knew if I did not get away from my master, I was already a dead man."

"I was my mistress's washerwoman," Sally said. "I have had one sadness after another. I brought seven children into the world and my master sold every last one away from me."

The man Jesse said nothing. He had a very hard, angry look. Later, Sally told me that in Georgia he had been an overseer. He looked to have as bad a temper as Sir. He traveled with his son, David, the other of the Littles.

"I am called Abraham," another man spoke up. I did mostly carpenter work for my master. I think myself to be thirty-six years of age. I had a wife and three children but they were sold away from me. My master hired me out over and often because of my woodworking skills."

When it was my turn, I did not know I would say so much. I told them of my escape from my mistress in Maryland and of my mother and how she loved to tell stories. I showed them my story quilt. I told them how she was taken to the Slave pen in Alexandria. I told them how I wish I could escape to freedom. "First," I said, "she was sent to a farm in Mississippi and then Kentucky."

Mistress Conductor said, "Across the river from Kentucky is Ohio. In Ohio are many ways north to Canada." This gave me hope. Maybe she can find her way to me in freedom. Then Mr. Tabbard asked that I say my mother's name again. I did so three times so it was most clear. There are so many strange and new things these days. It is the second full moon of this month of May.

Friday, June 1, 1855
Eastern Shores of Mary's Land, Dorchester County

I had a most wonderful dream. I called out my mother's name to Mother Wind again and again.

And then Mother Wind called out her name, too, the same way she called for her children to come on home. I pray my mother can hear her.

All day Mr. Tabbard talked to Harriet, who will lead us, also calling her Conductor as a sign of respect. I heard them discussing the Slave laws. These Friends who help us take a great risk and have powerful sore troubles. I say my Bible prayer so my fears lessen—*yea, though I walk through the valley of the shadow of death, I will fear no evil: for thou art with me*—but the fears are gnawing.

Mr. Tabbard and Mistress Conductor were huddled tonight and whispered for a long while. Then Mistress Conductor called us all to gather around. She looked at each one of us. After a long while, she finally spoke. "Your time for turning back is long past. We are moving toward your freedom now. We will get there. Fear not, for the Lord Almighty walks along with us." Everyone was silent, including the Little Ones. But everything inside me was a loud roar of sadness, and the tears came. It was the first time I felt how deep inside I hurt. I am leaving with no good-byes to anyone I love. Abbey will find out from Sir when he returns to Virginia that I have run away. I know she will worry, but I hope she will be happy for me. But I pray she will not fall sick as I did from the Shock, or if she does, someone will nurse her back to herself. Thinking of Abbey gives me such sorrow. “Rest,” Conductor Harriet said to all of us, but this night nobody knows how.

Along the Underground Railroad

June 2–July 10, 1855

Saturday, June 2, 1855
Eastern Shores of Mary's Land, Dorchester County

Late at night when the sky was mostly dark, everyone was bundled and ready to go. Abraham and Squire were told to move the large cabinet away from the wall. Underneath, the floorboards lifted up to reveal a door. We climbed down a stair ladder that led underground. Squire and Adam were first. Then Mistress Conductor climbed down. Sally and Nancy were next. Abraham lowered the Little One, then the Littler One. Then my turn, and Jesse was last.

A torch was lit on the wall. We followed this tunnel, which opened to another underground room. This connected to another underground passageway that was not lit. We walked down this dark underground tunnel a distance. "Move quickly," Mistress Conductor urged us. And we did, as fast as we could.

Adam and Squire carried the Littles on their backs so that we could make good time. It is hard to know how long we traveled this way under the ground. I was happy not to be alone. After a long while, the sound of water lapping against the land was heard up ahead. Mistress Conductor told us to stop. We were at the end of the tunnel.

Mistress instructed us to stay inside. Then she

motioned for Abraham to follow. Before I took another breath, they had disappeared into the night; my heart pounded in my ears. Abraham returned. And soon we heard the quick footsteps of the Conductor behind. "Keep moving," she told us in a strong voice.

We each stepped out into the dark. There was the smell of rain mixed with salty, marshy air. But rain did not come. Summer insects had already begun to swarm.

Sunday, June 3, 1855
Eastern Shores of Mary's Land, Dorchester County

In the daytime, I had no appetite for food. Resting was not easy. Mistress Conductor made sure we were truly hid under fallen trees and covered among the bushes or leaves. It is Sunday, so no search teams would get organized until Monday. By then, maybe we would be so far from here. It surprised me that I could sleep. And as soon as night fell, we walked again, stepping fast as we could. And the rain stepped along with us. I write in my journal whenever I can, whenever we stop and there is enough light and I am not too tired. It is not easy, but I need my companion. My writing book is my only true friend left, it seems.

Thursday, June 7, 1855
Eastern Shores of Mary's Land, Dorchester County

Night was as dark as pitch. Through marshy places where water overtook the land, there was only the sound of wind and water. Sally had a mighty fear of snakes, and walking through marshy areas made it hard on everyone. She hesitated, jumped, and almost screamed twice. Mistress Conductor cautioned her that she must keep silent. Squire offered to carry her if need be. But she would not allow it. I think she did this mostly to be brave for her boy.

When we came to a certain place, Mistress Conductor told us to sleep if we could. It was still night, but we had run out of road to walk on. I wondered what would happen next. There was only water up ahead of us. I was sad for no more land. It seemed like the end of the world, but everyone was glad to stop.

"Chesapeake." Abraham was the first to speak. "That is the Chesapeake Bay," he said, breathing deeply the marshy air. Night birds sang out. Others answered it. A soft breeze blew across us. The night was so clear; the sky was so full of stars.

"Look-y there," Squire whispered. He was speaking to everyone but especially the Little Ones. "Look." He pointed up. "Look at all the twinkling stars. See that?" Squire pointed. Everyone was wide-eyed and quiet. "They call that bunch of stars the Drinking Gourd," he said. "They look like a dipping cup. Do you see that one, the way it is shining so bright? That is the biggest one of all. That is our star—it is called the North Star. We will follow it all the way north. It stays shining up in the sky all night long, to bring luck."

I listened, too. I remembered a favorite story from my story quilt. I heard my mother's voice with every word and I told it this way:

Back at the beginning of the world, everything was black as pitch. Light had not been made yet to sit up in the sky. There was no blazing sun, no glowing moon, and no stars. The only light was fire that came from the center of the earth.

There was a village at the beginning of the world. The first people lived there. There was a mother and father and a girl. They knew how to get to that fire. They cooked their food with that fire. It kept them warm. These people had to do everything to make the world—grow the trees and grass, step out the valleys, build up the mountains, hollow out the catching places for water to fill the oceans and seas. They made the animals that live in all places. One morning when the girl woke, she came to the warmth of the fire. She smelled potatoes roasting. She could see the white and red flames of the fire. "Eat!" the mother said. While she ate the roasted potatoes, she thought about how you could not tell when there was morning and when there was night. When she became full, she knew what to do. She grabbed hold of the hottest part of the fire and tossed it into the sky. This is how the sun was placed to blaze in the sky. Next she threw a glowing potato into the sky. This became the moon. Then she grabbed the burning ashes and threw those up into the sky. Then the girl stepped up into the sky and made her way across. Where she walked, she sprinkled the ashes across the dark sky. The Star Road was made.

That is the path made by the girl at the beginning of the world, the girl who threw the bright sparks of fire high up into the sky to make a light road through darkness. She laid the path of stars in the heavens to show our way north.

As I wrote the story in my journal to always have it just this way, Squire spoke to me. "You told it right fine, Miss Eliza." He smiled at me. "You told it mighty fine, indeed." I felt proud inside. I knew my mother, Jane Mae, would be proud, too.

Later, three new shadows rowed up in boats. I wondered if this was our capture. The man in the first boat steered toward us—no one breathed or moved. Then the man spoke. His voice was as deep as the black water. "A Friend of a Friend sends me."

"God bless you," the Conductor replied. Those were the safety words Mistress Conductor must hear. This meant these were trusted Friends here to help us. We had to stay off main roads. Slave catchers and their tracking dogs and maybe Sir might be waiting for us on roads. But they would never think we would travel by boat. Besides, a scent is lost in the water; dogs would lose the trail. That was why Old Joe sent me along the river stream to the first safe house. Suddenly my insides felt like starry wind. "You think we ought to be able to make Wilmington by daylight?" the Conductor asked.

"I reckon that we will have to," the first boatman said.

"Delaware," said another. The men divided between the boats. We needed many hands rowing. The feel of smooth water moving under me put me at peace and I fell to sleep at once. I did not wake even to be loaded into a wagon. We were carried to the next safe station house. It was morning when we arrived. That meant we could rest more.

Safe House No. 2 / Wilmington, Delaware

Sunday, June 10, 1855
Wilmington, Delaware

This safe house is a plain clapboard house. Here we met more Friends of Friends. The Friend of this house is a most kind man. We are to stay another three days. The man paid the cost for proper bedding, clothing, and shoes. I am grateful to Doe, who gave me my first pair of hard-soled boots.

I learned every person in our group is bound to St. Catharines, which is in Ontario, Canada, but not the freedman in our group, Mr. Adam Will. He shall go to his home in Rochester, New York, where his family waits for him. They have legal papers that show he is a free man.

While in this safe house, Mr. Adam Will is so jolly and full of talk with everyone. He told us of being kidnapped and the bad treatment he suffered. "But I would not give up hope. I used my laughing spirit and wits to escape," he said, chuckling to the room full of people. "Looking back on things, you could say I ran away as quick as Mr. Rabbit did from old Mr. Wolf's lair." Then Mr. Will looked at me and pointed to the bundle that was my quilt, which was nearby. He gave me a tip of his head and a wink with his eye. He told our new friends, "We have a storyteller in our group." He smiled all around and pointed to me. I hesitated at first, but one nod from the Conductor gave me faith to continue. Everyone huddled around, and I told the story this way, as I remember to write it:

Wolf always took the best planting ground and gave Rabbit the briars. Wolf planted corn. Rabbit couldn't plant a thing. So all winter Rabbit had to live on Wolf's corn. Wolf told his wife, "I do not know why I cannot grow good corn. I got the best growing ground for myself, but my stalks yield no corn."

"Next year do not plant corn," his wife said. "Next year plant peanuts."

The next year Wolf did just the same by Rabbit as the year before, taking the best soil, and he did not plant corn. But now Wolf's peanut crop was dropping off. When he went to look at his peanut patch, he saw deep tracks. "Something is getting into my peanut patch before I can," he said. I'm going to make a scarecrow to scare that thief off."

That night Rabbit came with his harvest bags. He saw the scarecrow Wolf had put up. When he got close enough to touch it, he could see it was just a bundle of rags. Rabbit filled his sacks and went home. "That scarecrow is not scary at all," Wolf said. "I will fix that rascal once and for all." So Wolf made another scarecrow, this time out of tar.

When Rabbit came again, he saw the tar baby. "Tsk, tsk, tsk," Rabbit said. "Has old Wolf set up another scarecrow?" Rabbit had never seen anything like that before. He went close enough and touched it. His paw stuck good and tight. Rabbit let out a holler. He tried to pry his hand away with his other hand. That was his second mistake. He used his right foot and that got stuck. Next morning, when Wolf saw Rabbit all tangled up, he laughed. "I finally got you," he told Rabbit.

"Please, friend Wolf, let me go. I will never bother your crops again." But Wolf just laughed.

"Brer Wolf," Rabbit begged. "Please oh please, do right by me. You may roast me, you may toast me, you may cut me up and you may eat me, but please, whatever you do, do not toss me in the briar patch. That will surely be the end of me!"

"That is the very thing I aim to do with you!" Wolf said. And one, two, three, Mr. Fly can sit on my knee, Wolf tossed Rabbit into the briars. Rabbit laughed and stomped his feet. "You should know by now. All my family was born and bred in briars. We can escape them easily. That is what made me tell

you to throw me in there!" And Rabbit scampered away.

Wolf went home to his wife dragging his tail. "No rabbit soup for dinner," he said. "I'll try to catch him another day."

Mr. Will thanked me most graciously. "What shall you do when you get to freedom, Miss Eliza?" he asked. "Whatever you do, I am sure you will do it well and be a success." This gave me so much joy, to hear such fine words from a freed man. He said this in front of everyone and it made me feel free.

Safe House No. 3 / Chester, Pennsylvania

Thursday, June 14, 1855
Chester, Pennsylvania

"Move, move, move!" Mistress Conductor urged. I did, as fast as I could. She told us, "Do not ever look back. There is nothing behind you. Keep your eyes ahead toward freedom."

Squire said to me with a big grin, "I keep my sight planted north." I was glad I did not have to worry which is the right way to go. Mistress Conductor knows the way.

Day after day something new happens. Nothing is the same. There are many new Friends and places. Sometimes we journey walk in the day, but most times we journey walk at night. Every time, we walk as far as possible to go. Sunrise. Moonrise. Sunrise. No moon. Days and nights pass. It is all the same. Now we've come to another safe house. This is in a free state, Pennsylvania, but maybe it is not so free.

We were told that patrollers, Slave catchers, were everywhere along the way to our next safe house. This fact alone makes worry stick to my insides like cockleburs. For safety we changed our route plan. This will mean a delay, but maybe we'll have safe quarters. Living outside in the elements is hard company on us all but especially for the Little Ones. My hope to stop and rest is more for them. I miss their laughter along the way.

Friday, June 15, 1855
Philadelphia, Pennsylvania

Word came that Philadelphia was safe after all. The journey there was a short one. Normally, we go by foot at night, but this time we traveled by wagon and in broad daylight to the next safe house.

Safe House No. 4 / Philadelphia, Pennsylvania

Saturday, June 16, 1855
Philadelphia, Pennsylvania

We have reached the Philadelphia safe house. There was a gathering and a welcome full of Friends. All hearts lit up the room. The Friend in this house gave us much hope. He said in due time, we would safely arrive through Freedom's Gate: Canada.

This evening, eleven carriages arrived. This was Meeting Night. Everyone gathered to the meeting hall. There was much happiness that we are safe. But there was caution as well. Normally Pennsylvania is a free state, but now the enforcement of the Slave laws make it terrible for the poor Slaves or anyone who helps them. Some of these Friends are watched. I am full of worry for us all. But mostly for Mr. Adam Will, who is already free.

From the talk of Abraham, the Slave catcher dogs may be a worse capture than any master. Mistress

Conductor said, "Think only of freedom—that's the only thought to have." I worked hard not to worry. Sally stood near me. A hand on a shoulder is a comfort. "I want my freedom, Eliza," Sally said. "I want my freedom." I prayed we all might have it.

Sunday, June 17, 1855
Philadelphia, Pennsylvania

We were fed a great feast of black-eyed peas with pieces of fatback and skillet bread. There was barley and corn soup and, my favorite, roast mutton.

Every one of the Friends spoke of the Good Book. They talked of things that I have read. That night my ears grew in size. I heard so much. I counted that our host said "Promised Land" at least five times. Then he asked, "Is it not better to die in the wilderness than to serve the Egyptians?" And I knew he was speaking of Moses. It brought me hope, that the Moses of our people was also leading us.

That night the menfolk were moved to a secret place, to be hid in the property barn. We women were moved through a secret door that led up to the walls inside the attic of this safe house. Mistress Conductor said it is best that Silas and David stay to the house with the women, until it is time to move on again.

Wednesday, June 20, 1855
Philadelphia, Pennsylvania

Tomorrow we are to start our journey again, but something happened tonight that frightened me to my teeth. From the little attic window I saw one of the Friends we had met on our arrival come to the door. He knocked the secret knock. But no one answered him. He knocked again, hard enough not to be paying a friendly visit. Something inside me said that if he meant to do harm, he would have knocked the door down by now. But he steadily called out to our host and kept knocking. Sally and Nancy slept.

The man continued to knock. Then I decided what I would do. Through the secret passageway I came down to the door, careful not to open it. In my best way I said, "Yes, may I help you?"

At first there was silence. I thought the Friend had gone. Then he said "The wind blows from the south today" three times, and I heard his footsteps run. I knew this was a warning that bounty hunters were near. I was surprised that I acted as though I had no fear in the knowledge of this, but I was afraid. I knew I must wait and watch until our host and guide returned. They would know what we must do. So I decided to wait for their return. On my way back to the secret passageway I heard approaching footsteps and voices. Then came another knock. It was not the knock of the Friends. It was too dangerous to go back to the secret attic place to wait. Before I could get back up the stairs, someone began opening the door to the meeting house. I had to protect the Littles and Sally and Nancy, who were sleeping above. There was a wardrobe close to where I stood. As the door to the meeting house opened, I had just enough time to climb inside the wardrobe unnoticed. I prayed no one detected my hiding place. I heard three people walk into the room. They moved around as if they were searching for something. Then I heard another person enter the meeting house. Thankfully, it was our host. I heard him greet the men and inquire if they were lost. Quickly he ushered them from the house. I climbed out of the wardrobe and ran to our hiding place in the attic.

I thought I was the only one who had heard the commotion. But I was not. The Little Ones heard it, too. When I returned to the safety of the attic, big round eyes followed me around the room. "Sleep," I whispered softly. But they came to my sleeping place instead. My story quilt spread out on my pallet, I said in my most cheerful way, "Do you want to know the story of how a little boy named David fought a giant named Goliath?" And I pointed to the picture panel on my quilt. I remembered and I write it this way:

Jesse had eight sons. The youngest was a shepherd named David. He sang and played the harp, too.

King Saul liked the shepherd boy so much, he had him carry his armor. When Saul heard David sing and play the harp, his bad mood left him. So David played music whenever King Saul had bad spirits. Around this same time Saul's enemies were causing the people a whole lot of trouble. There was one battle after another, and his enemies were winning. Saul's army was preparing for battle. The biggest and meanest of all the soldiers ran to the front of the line. He was ten feet tall, covered in the strongest armor from his head to his feet. He had a sword and he had a shield. He could have easily killed fifty men all at once. His name was Goliath.

David told the king, "With the help of the Lord, I can destroy this giant."

Saul did not think a boy could do that even with the Lord on his side. But of all things, David was not afraid. He had already faced danger two times before. Once, he had used his slingshot to kill a great bear; another time he killed a lion that had gone after his father's sheep. David went to the river to pray. He chose five smooth stones from the riverbed and put them into his leather pouch.

Goliath said, "Send me somebody to fight!" All at once, Goliath looked down to see David standing there. It looked to Goliath that he was alone. "I want to fight a man—no, ten men—no, fifty men, and you send me a boy!" The giant pounded his chest. He stomped the ground with his heavy feet. Then he unleashed all his anger onto David.

David wasn't even a little bit afraid. He reached into his pouch. He took one of the stones, placed it in his slingshot, and hurled it at Goliath. The stone landed right in the middle of the giant's forehead, the one place on his whole body his shiny armor did not cover. Goliath fell dead to the ground. The whole world must have stopped turning long enough to see that little boy David kill that giant Goliath.

Mama told me this story whenever I felt most afraid. Late in the night when Mistress Conductor returned, I told her the news of the night visitors. She listened all the way through my telling. "Do not be fretful now. Sleep," she said. But Sir's big boots followed me in my dreams all night long.

Thursday, June 21, 1855
Philadelphia, Pennsylvania

Squire was right; a lucky star was shining down on us. We traveled to the next safe house by wagon, eluding the bounty hunters. And so many changes had taken place on this freedom road since the Conductor had come this way last. Now there was a faster way to freedom: a train. The Northern Central Railway finished laying the tracks from Williamsport, Pennsylvania, all the way to Elmira, New York. Once we could reach Elmira, freedom in Canada was next.

The stationmaster in Elmira was a former Slave also. He had found his way to freedom; now he was a helping Friend to others. If we could get to Williamsport in time, we could ride on the four o'clock train! No dogs, Slave catchers, or Sir could beat that!

We must leave for Williamsport now and we must hurry. It will take two or three days to get there on foot.

Friday, June 22, 1855
Philadelphia, Pennsylvania

We left for Williamsport and the train station before noon. But we went in disguise in a furniture wagon. Potato sacks and parcels of hams were to be loaded onto the wagon. But those bags were not filled with potatoes or hams. They were filled with us. We were the human cargo. We each received a potato sack and were told to climb into it. Abraham and Squire were to ride with Mr. Porter Nelson as hired help. They were pretending to deliver a wagonload of potatoes and hams to the Williamsport train. All along the way I prayed. *Please, God, make a way for us to pass. Just as you parted the sea for Moses and his people, let us go safely into the Promised Land. Even if I still must think on Sir, let me do it in freedom now.*

Safe House No. 5 / Williamsport, Pennsylvania

Monday, June 25, 1855
Williamsport, Pennsylvania

We are not staying long in this safe house. It is very close to the train station.

Nancy and Sally were so full with talk to me. Their happy feelings showed. "We are close to freedom now!" They almost cried with hugging me. I wanted to join in their happiness, but I could not. "What is wrong, Eliza?" Sally asked. But I could not rightly say. Too many thoughts of people I miss, plus dreams that never let me rest. Sir's boots thunder-walking steadily closer to me. I try hard not to fear, but it is stronger. "We all have something to make us afraid.

But, Eliza, you must try to be happy in your freedom in spite of that," Sally said.

North Central Railway Station
Williamsport, Pennsylvania

Tuesday, June 26, 1855
Williamsport, Pennsylvania

We arrived at the station early in the day. The Friends of the Elmira stationmaster were there to meet us. Abraham and Squire lifted our sacks from the wagon and gently placed us in the baggage car of the train. They stacked us behind and among the trunks, personal belongings, and boxes of the travelers with tickets. We did not have to be told to stay hid at least until the train started to move. I crouched down and pulled the coarse sack apart to make a better breathing hole, but it was little help. It was a very hot day. The baggage car is located right behind the engine. This made the temperature hotter still. I thought of the day so long ago when I rode the train for the first time with Mistress Margaret. Though the train car with Mistress

Margaret was fine and so much more comfortable than this, I was happier for this train ride.

The train conductor was sympathetic to our cause. He did not demand payment or a ticket. But still, he warned us we must stay hidden. "This car will be a very hot and noisy ride," he said. "But you should arrive safely in Elmira by morning."

Normal paying passengers are not allowed here in this wide-open, empty car. There are no windows but two big doors on either side. There is one other door that leads to the engine car. High and low shelves are all around for mail cargo and smaller baggage.

Suddenly the train conductor's voice gave the signal to move. "All aboard."

Once the train was in fast motion we could stretch and move around. I wanted to get out of my sack and was grateful for the hot breeze that blew through the window.

When the train made a station stop, we ran back to our sacks. Passenger baggage was collected, unloaded, or loaded. When the train started up again, we came out of hiding. The farther we went, the more the car emptied. Soon, there was lots of room to move around.

While the train moved down the track, the men were full of talk. "The only way we can gain our freedom is to fight for it," Squire said.

"What good would fighting do? Someone bigger will come along and you would have to fight him, too," Jesse said.

"You have to fight power with power!" Adam Will said. "But you should use wisdom." They talked of the ways to get the whole business of Slavery to end. The two Littles played with packing string they had found in the baggage car. Sally and Nancy and Mistress Conductor joined in no discussion. They sat on a storage trunk alone in their own thoughts.

Then Jesse laughed. His voice was loud as a drum over the roar of the engine. Up until now, he was most quiet through this whole journey. "Where is our storyteller?" he asked. "Tell us a happy story, Eliza," he said. And I decided on this one:

Once upon a long time ago, rain did not fall for nearly about a whole year. The crops were doing badly. The animals were hot and hungry and thirsty. Creator did not want his children to starve, so he created a field. In the middle of the field was one large tree full of every good kind of ripe and juicy fruit. Tiger got there first and claimed it for himself.

"Stay away from here," he growled, "or I will eat you up!" And he made the animals pick the fruit off the tree for him. Before long, Spider came by as

hungry and thirsty as the next animal. They all knew Spider was small, but they knew he was wise. The animals told Spider all their troubles.

Spider made a plan. The next morning all of the animals came for a secret meeting in the forest near where Tiger was sleeping. When he woke up, he asked, "Where are my workers? I need these fruits picked."

Just then Spider ran past. "Oh, Tiger, forgive them. If you going to be upset with anyone, be upset with me. I had to tie all the animals to the trees. I have a great rope that none can escape from; now all the animals will be safe."

Tiger knew Spider to be wise. "Tell me why you have done this."

"For their own good. A big wind is coming. And it will blow everything off the earth! I have seen it done. Tiger, you must run."

Just then the animals in the forest began to make a great racket. Eagle and Stork and Owl and all the birds flapped their wings. They caused the leaves to shake and twist. Elephant and Ox and Otter and Crocodile and all the animals on the ground beat on the hollow logs and smacked the trees. They scurried around in the brush and altogether set the entire forest to swinging and swaying like it was the end of the world.

"What do I do?" Tiger cried.

"You must run!" Spider warned.

"You must tie me down, too," he pleaded. "I do not want the big wind to blow me off the earth. It is such a sweet place. Take pity on me."

"But you are big and powerful. You have a good chance of escaping alive!"

"Do as I say," Tiger growled. "Tie me down, Spider, or you shall regret this."

Spider tied the rope tight. But all the while Tiger shouted, "Tighter! Tighter!"

Once Tiger was tied up good and tight, Spider stepped back and looked at him. Then he called for the other animals to come out of the forest.

"Look here," Spider said. "Look here at the one who tried to keep all the fruit for himself instead of sharing it." And for once in his life, Tiger felt true shame and promised to change his ways. Then all of the animals sat in the shade of the big tree and happily feasted on the delicious fruit together. "Very well, then," Spider said. "Very well."

Jesse said, "Thank you, Eliza. And thank you for my boy's sake. All my life I am always in fright. Now it look to me like some of the fright is going away from me."

I was grateful for these words. And I told him so. And I wrote them down to have them always.

Wednesday, June 27, 1855
Elmira, New York

There was daylight in the sky when the train came to Elmira. We stayed in the baggage train car until a wagon came to fetch us. It was close to dark when the wagon arrived. The stars had started to show and twinkle. Squire smiled and pointed up at the North Star once again. "See," he said to the two boys, "it still shines the best."

Safe House No. 6 / Elmira, New York

Thursday, June 28, 1855
Elmira, New York

We arrived safely at the home of the safe house stationmaster in Elmira. The Conductor and he were so happy to see each other again. I feel like I could rest forever here. The stationmaster and his wife are very kind. They fed us as much as we wanted. And I ate as much as I could.

I do not know what I should be thinking. We are so

close to the end of the journey. Steadily I wonder what I will do when I finally gain my freedom. Who will tell me what is next for me in the world? I do not know.

Saturday, June 30, 1855
Elmira, New York

Sally says in freedom, I will be my own mistress. I think of my life so long ago with Abbey and how I miss her. I think of my mother and wonder how I could live free without her. Will I ever see her again? Ezekiel's words come to my mind from so long ago. And I think of what I was told at the first safe house. Across the river from Kentucky into Ohio are many roads to Canada and the Promised Land.

Monday, July 2, 1855
Elmira, New York

Whatever are the feelings of the Conductor, she does not show them to us. She appears to have her mind full of thoughts toward something only she can see. Inside me I feel like the buzz of a hive of bees. I can hardly sit myself still.

Safe House No. 7 / Rochester, New York

Friday, July 6, 1855,
Rochester, New York

We arrived at a new safe house in Rochester, New York, last night. Today we said good-bye to Adam Will. This morning, Mistress Conductor greeted each of us at the morning meal with prayers and a happy smile. Then she led us in singing.

There came a knock at the door. It was not the secret knock of a Friend. I wanted to run and hide, but there was no reason to. Our host boldly opened the door and invited in the guests, who appeared to be expected. There, walking across the threshold of the room, was a group of the most fine-looking people I had ever seen. Mr. Adam Will fell to his knees and put his tearful face in his hands. There before our very eyes he was rejoined to the bosom of his family. My heart was so glad for him.

It is hard to think but I am almost free.

The Falls
Straddling the Border Between Canada and the United States

Tuesday, July 10, 1855
On the road to St. Catharines

Everything looks brighter with almost-free eyes. But what I have seen today is hard to describe and most hard to say into words.

We came to a place where we heard a most mighty rush of thundering water. The ground under our feet trembled and shook. At first I thought there was going to be another earthquake. But it was raining and everything was covered in a spray from hurrying waters. It was not rain that fell from the sky but water that poured down from the river's level into the break below. These falling waters were called Niagara Falls. I stood looking at the almighty waters and thought of Moses and how God parted the seas for the Hebrew people. And I remembered my prayer that we shall be delivered into the Promised Land. This gave me a great feeling, thinking that now my prayers were answered in these falling waters. We stopped our journey to view the majesty of the waters lighted up and dazzling in the sun, the sky filled up with rainbows. It was strange that I felt so calm and peaceful inside, yet all around me were rolling, leaping, roaring, tumbling waters. And before nightfall, we crossed the river by ferry into Canada.

A New Journey Begins in Ontario

July 11–22, 1855

Safe at Last

Wednesday, July 11, 1855
St. Catharines, Canada

Crossing out of Uncle Sam's land, Mistress Conductor said, "Well, children, now you are free." A feeling came over us all just as the rushing waters hit the river. Upon hearing those words, Jesse picked up his boy, David, and hugged him through tears. Abraham fell to his knees. Squire grabbed Sally by her waist and swung her around. And the words echoed in my heart like a dream.

When we arrived, Friends of the Conductor met us. We were taken to a church building to rest. In the morning, we are to be taken to a boarding house where we will live until permanent quarters are found. The men of our group go the men's boarding house next door. Behind the house is a great field of green grass. It was a sight to see former Slaves as free people walking with confidence out in the open air. And there were white people, too, who do not threaten or cause fear, but live side by side with former Slaves. And not one or the other was mistreated, whipped, or forced to work. What would my old master and mistress think if they were to see this?

Our Conductor is a great woman. Wherever she goes, she is held up for all her great goodness. I see what she does and I am sure she is driven by a power from the Almighty himself. Twice a year, she journeys south in Uncle Sam's country to bring people out of bondage. She is fearless. I do not think I could ever be as fearless as that to return. And there is the stationmaster. It is he who arranged for our safe and speedy journey by train. And all of the Friends along the way. These are good ways to show how to live free. But what will be my freedom way?

Today I think again of my old mistress and have only sadness for her. And for missing Abbey and for my mother, Jane Mae. Then my thoughts turn to Sir. But the worry thoughts seem so far away from me now. I remember my last day in Virginia. It comes to me like the falling waters of Niagara.

I remember the day Sir stood before me and I did something a Slave should never do. I looked at Sir right in his hard gray eyes. All along this freedom way I have worried and wondered on this. But now I understand and it is clear to me. The reason I saw Sir's eyes is that just as I had grown taller than Abbey, I had also grown to be as tall as Sir, even while he wore his big boots. Now almost a year has passed and I am probably taller still. I remember a story my mother would tell when Sir was his meanest. But when she told it, the story made her laugh so much. Now I see the joke was on Sir, after all. And I write it here to remember it:

The Knee-High Man lived deep in the swamp. All he wanted in the world that he knew was to be bigger than he was. Sometimes he'd look up to the sky and see the moon move from a sliver of light to a round glowing ball. "If the moon can grow bigger, how can I?" Knee-High Man began to give this more and more thought every day.

One day he saw Bre Horse romping around his fields. I wish I was as big as Horse, *he thought. Knee-High Man decided to ask Horse how he could become bigger like him. And Bre Horse told him. "I eat corn all day. I run around." Knee-High Man decided to try that. But he did not grow bigger. He got a big stomachache and had to rub his legs with liniment oil.*

Next he saw Bre Bull. He asked Bre Bull how he could make himself as strong as he was. Bre Bull told him what to do. But Knee-High Man did not like the taste of grass, he bellowed so loud his throat got sore, and he snorted so much his nostrils burned. And the Knee-High Man was not any bigger.

After a while he heard old Mr. Hoot Owl in the swamp. Mr. Hoot Owl had big round eyes. Everyone thought he looked wise. Knee-High Man climbed up into Mr. Hoot Owl's tree to see if the owl could help him figure out how to grow bigger in size. "Why do you want to get bigger in the first place? You are made the way you are."

"But what about when I get into a fight? Would you want me to win it?"

"But has anybody ever picked a fight with you?"

"Well, no, not early and not lately."

"Well, you do not have any reason to be bigger than you are for fighting purposes."

"No, not if you put it like that." Knee-High Man thought some more. "But I want to be able to see a long way." Just then, there was a great noise on the other side of the swamp. Knee-High Man's head jerked in the direction of the noise. Bre Bear had caught three fish at once. "Did you see that?" Knee-High said to Mr. Hoot Owl.

"You sure can see a long way off."

"But that's from up in this tree."

"And your size makes it easy for you to climb a tree. You know, you do not have any real reason to be bigger in your body, but you sure do have a lot of reasons to grow bigger in your brain."

This gave me a hearty laugh. I looked at my quilt and thought of the love my dear mother, Jane Mae, has for me and the wisdom of the stories she told me.

Monday, July 16, 1855
St. Catharines, Canada

This morning, I woke up with a feeling that joy was all around me because of the most wonderful dream I had. In the dream, a line was drawn on the ground. I was standing on one side of the line. On the other was a beautiful log cabin sitting out in a field of green grass. Flowers were bunched up all over the land. Singing surrounded me, too. Bells rang out. Near the cabin was a beautiful lady. I was sure it was my mother, though I could not see her clearly enough. But the lady stretched her hand out to reach me. I thought, *How can I reach her?* And I knew I must. I tried and fell. I stood and moved toward her. Then she spread out a beautiful hand-stitched quilt on the grassy green ground. I tried again to reach her. And I fell again, but this time I landed right in the middle of the quilt while the singing wind blew all around me. And that is when I awoke.

By the time I got dressed, Jesse, Squire, and Abraham had already risen and were in search of work. Sally, Nancy, the Littles, and I walked back to the boarding house from our morning search. Good news for Nancy. She has found housing and a position. Sally and Nancy talked happily along the way, but I did not join the talk. We carry our bundles with us, as today could be the lucky day that we also find permanent position work.

When we got back to the boarding house, I saw someone at the other end of the street that looked familiar. It was a beautiful lady like the lady in my dream. I wanted to speak to her. I looked carefully at the woman. This woman was tall but not so tall. She was lean but not so lean. Yet she looked like someone I knew. The woman began waving in my direction. *Could she be waving at me?* I wondered.

Then this woman started to walk toward me. The closer she got to me, the faster she walked.

I tucked my quilt bundle under my arm and started walking quickly toward her. Then she started running. And I did too. The woman did something that made me stop. She said my name aloud: "Eliza."

I could see by the look of her eyes. I could see by the smooth color of her skin and by her beautiful face, this was not a dream. This was real. This was my dream come true. The woman opened her arms wide and flung them around me. My eyes flooded with tears. Everything was a blur. And only then, when I felt her soft arms surround me, I knew who she was. I felt her love. I looked down at my quilt bundle and could see that my little compass arrow was steadily pointed north, directly at her. It fixed in my mind what I knew. This was my mother, Jane Mae.

"I knew I would find you," my mother, Jane Mae, said. "I never gave up hope."

Saturday, July 21, 1855
St. Catharines, Canada

In the boarding house there are many children. I will begin my new life in freedom teaching others how to read and write. I will do as my former mistress did for me. I am sharing my gift and it makes me glad. But it will be a gift to share in the broad light of day, not a secret.

First I will teach them the shapes and sounds of letters. Then I will teach them to arrange the letters into words. I will show them ways to remember their lessons very easily. Then I will show them how to read the groups of words. And I will remind them each day of the kind regard I have for them to learn. "This is your inheritance," I will tell them. "This is your insurance for your freedom. This is the way you live free." As Old Joe said, "Eliza, you can read and write. . . . That makes you bigger than even the man who tries to keep you a Slave."

Sunday, July 22, 1855
St. Catharines, Canada

There is one page left in my writing book. Here I must remember how I spent my first true day in freedom. I found a patch of sweet green grass. I spread out my quilt, just as the beautiful lady did in my dream days ago. When I spread it out, I saw all the story pictures. And I saw the empty places. And I remembered that I must finish it now. And I know how I am going to finish my quilt. The eleventh panel will be stitched with roads that twist and turn and lead to the blue satin cloth of the great waterfalls of Niagara. This panel will show the story of my journey. In the last panel, I will stitch a picture of my book. This panel will tell the whole story.

Author's Note

Eliza's Freedom Road: An Underground Railroad Diary began as a collection of my favorite stories and folktales retold by me. But as I began to construct the collection, a storyteller's voice emerged: a young slave girl named Eliza. It is Eliza's point of view that shaped the stories I would tell. But then came the question: Who gave these stories to her? The answer was simple: a loving parent, of course.

Eliza's Freedom Road: An Underground Railroad Diary is a work of fiction. It is the account of a young slave girl's escape journey to freedom and Canada through the Underground Railroad system. Eliza lived during the nineteenth-century slave trade in our country. We hear of Eliza and her life from 1854 to 1855 through her journal. It is impossible to confirm or verify any one specific route taken on the Underground Railroad, as it was often not the same route for reasons of safety and circumstance. Voice and capitalization are as they would have been in a journal of that time. Great care was taken with factual details.

This story draws much of its inspiration from a constant theme in human experience: the act of traveling to go to a better way of life. This theme shows itself in the earliest stories of human experience; it directs our drive for freedom and is part of our personal heritage. It seemed correct to focus these retellings as a travel journey.

Here the inspiration of other literature spurred me on, specifically, *The Canterbury Tales* by Geoffrey Chaucer written in the fourteenth century. *The Canterbury Tales* is a journey story made for religious experience, a pilgrimage. Those fourteenth-century travelers had a different reason and motivation to tell stories for their journey, but it was still a good jumping-off point for Eliza.

I believe the world turns upon a story. And it is a telling of how things came to be. Furthermore, I believe each of us—our lives—is a story that shapes the world. Stories give us hopeful messages that move us to feel and see, dream and act on what could ever be in the world. And these stories connect us all. I present some of my favorite ones here.

"THE COW-TAIL SWITCH," PAGES 10-12

Stories from West Africa are usually about kings, warriors, hunters, and the animals that populate their world. Stories are also told that explain how the world came to be. "The Cow-Tail Switch" is a story from Liberia based on a parable. When teaching stories like these were performed, the audience was asked to participate.

In actuality, a cow-tail switch is equal to a flyswatter. The holder would use it to brush flies away. But it is an elaborate and highly decorated object, ornamented and beautified with cowry shells. It is a symbol of authority and is highly prized. The chief of the tribe or the leader of the dance gets the honor of holding it. I especially like this story because it simply illustrates a very valuable lesson: A person is not dead unless he is truly forgotten. Or, value or rewards are given to those who remember their ancestors.

"WHY THERE ARE WHITE CAPS ON THE WATER," PAGES 18-20

The stories of how things got started or how the world was created are very popular because they explain how the world came to be. There are many versions and variants of every question we have about how the world was shaped. This story can be found in Zora Neale Hurston's collection *Mules and Men*, which is a book of Negro folklore written at a time when not much attention was given to the lives of Negroes (black people) and their social life. Zora Neale Hurston was a pioneer who traveled through the South in the 1930s compiling the stories, songs, children's games, and traditions of black life. The stories were written in heavy dialect. In her introduction she talks about how she had heard these stories as a child growing up in Eatonville, Florida. "Why There Are White Caps on the Water" is an angry and sad story, but I hope I have softened the blow.

"The Rooster and the Fox," pages 51-52

Of all folklore, beast tales and trickster tales (usually about a small animal who uses cleverness or mischief to overturn the social order to outwit and cheat death) are the most common and the most fun. In these fables, animals and birds speak and behave as humans. These stories were originally told to teach a lesson about human nature and behavior. In his original form, Reynard the fox was a medieval trickster with very few good qualities. All the animals inhabiting his world, including Chanticleer the rooster, could give a firsthand telling of misfortune when they encountered him. Here in this retelling, the tables are turned and fox has met his match.

In *Negro Myths from the Georgia Coast told in the Vernacular* by Charles C. Jones Jr., Chanticleer the rooster works with the fox to take revenge on a yellow rooster.

"Moses," pages 62-64

Moses was the son of Amram and Jochebed. He was the servant and an instrument of God. It is through Moses that God reveals the first five books of the Bible: Genesis, Exodus, Leviticus, Numbers, and Deuteronomy. And it is Moses who actually wrote them down. In the Exodus story we see firsthand how God uses Moses to free the children of Israel.

Throughout my childhood this story was an inspiration to me. I never grew tired of hearing of Moses's heart and bravery, and how he could lay down his life for the good of others. The Moses story was also inspiration for my folktale *Big Jabe* (HarperCollins, 2000). Through this story, Moses has grown to be more than a man. He is a symbol. It is no wonder Harriet Tubman was also considered Moses of Her People.

"The Flying People," pages 86-88

Telling the story of flying people will perhaps never grow old. There is magic and spiritualism inherent in the idea of becoming light enough to leave behind the burdens of this world to go to a better place. "The People Could Fly" is perhaps the most favorite and compelling story in this collection of favorite tales. It was made widely popular by Virginia Hamilton in her collection of folktales, *The People Could Fly*. It is a most extraordinarily magical tale of how hope and inspiration can be the strength you lean on for survival. It is no wonder that Eliza would tell this story when she is alone in the woods. Here she is able to transform her painful memories and present worries.

This also appears in Langston Hughes and Arna Bontemps's collection, *The Book of Negro Folklore*. It also was referred to in the Georgia Writers' Project, *Drums and Shadows,* which was a collection of oral folklore assembled during the 1930s.

"How Stars Came into the Sky," pages 105-106

It is natural and normal for human beings to wonder how and why. Creation stories fulfill this very human desire. In most instances it is chance or trickery that tells us how something in the world came to be. I had never come across a story about a girl who willfully participated in the creation of some part of the world until I found this story from the Bushmen in *Specimens of Bushman Folklore* by W. H. I. Bleek and L. C. Lloyd.

"The Rabbit, the Wolf, and the Tar Baby," pages 109-111

A good story has good strong legs. It never sits down and never stops moving. And it travels fast, like the wind. And like the wind it is difficult to say from where it comes. There is speculation that "The Tar Baby and The Rabbit Story" could have originated in India or Africa. Nevertheless, this is probably the most widely known of all the folktales. There are perhaps more than three hundred versions of this story. It was made popular by Joel Chandler Harris's collection of Uncle Remus stories. Humorous stories and trickster tales are all throughout the canon of African-American folklore. But often it was humor with a very clever bite.

"David and Goliath," pages 117-118

The popular story of "David and Goliath" is taken from the Bible, the book of Samuel. The idea to have the courage to stand up seemingly alone to insurmountable obstacles shows up time and time again in our modern day television shows, movies, and books. It continues to inspire us. It is no wonder that as a child this was another favorite of mine. "David and Goliath" tells of how even the young and not powerful can be chosen to face giant obstacles and can be given the greatest reward. The Bible story of the small boy David facing the giant Goliath leaves us with big lessons: We are powerful beyond measure even though on first impression we may appear puny, weak, and small. And it is not our physical size that moves obstacles out of our way. Rather, it is the size of the courage, belief, and faith inside of our hearts that stretches us beyond our own understandings. It is how we are able to boldly stand up to a fear as big as a giant, see it for what it is, and overcome it through faith in ourselves.

"Tiger and the Big Wind" pages 123-125

No gathering of folktales would be complete without Anansi. Here is Anansi the West African spider god, another of the tricksters. Compared to the other animals, he is not the strongest of beasts. He is small. He has no fangs or teeth. In order to survive, he has to be very cunning, wise, and clever. Anansi is a cultural hero who can do the most amazing things. He can turn around the social order of things. He can create wealth out of thin air. Anansi is even wise enough to own all stories.

The Anansi tales reflect the spirit of rebellion. Anansi the spider can do anything he sets his mind to, and do it very well. In most of the Anansi tales he is looking out for his number one fan, himself. But this time, Anansi shows his softer side and helps others. No one, Anansi included, likes a selfish and greedy bully.

This story is based on William Faulkner's retelling, which was told to him by a former slave from Virginia, Simon Brown. Simon Brown lived in a section of Columbia, South Carolina, around 1900 and was employed by William Faulkner's mother.

"The Knee-High Man," pages 134-135

Some stories and folktales are told to help us see the big picture. They may explain the unexplainable and they make us laugh at ourselves. "The Knee-High Man" is just that kind of story. There are a variety of stories based on this delightful folktale. A version of this story can be found in Roger D. Abrahams's book *Afro-American Folktales* and in Harold Courlander's book *A Treasury of Afro-American Folklore.*

Bibliography

• Books •

Abrahams, Roger D., ed. *Afro-American Folktales: Stories from Black Traditions in the New World.* New York: Pantheon Books, 1985.

Berlin, Ira. *Many Thousands Gone: The First Two Centuries of Slavery in North America.* Cambridge: The Belknap Press of Harvard University Press, 1998.

Blassingame, John W. *The Slave Community: Plantation Life in the Antebellum South.* New York: Oxford University Press, 1979.

Bleek, W. H. I., and L. C. Lloyd. *Specimens of Bushman Folklore.* London: George Allen & Company, 1911.

Botkin, B. A. *A Treasury of Southern Folklore: Stories, Ballads, Traditions, and Folkways of the People of the South.* New York: Crown Publishers, 1949.

———, ed. *Lay My Burden Down: A Folk History of Slavery.* New York: Delta, 1994.

Chaucer, Geoffrey. *The Canterbury Tales.* New York: Washington Square Press, 1971.

Courlander, Harold, ed. *A Treasury of Afro-American Folklore: The Oral Literature, Traditions, Recollections, Legends, Tales, Songs, Religious Beliefs, Customs, Sayings and Humor of Peoples of African Descent in the Americas.* New York: Marlowe & Company, 1976.

Davis, Charles T., and Henry Louis Gates Jr., eds. *The Slave's Narrative.* New York: Oxford University Press, 1985.

Dorson, Richard M., comp. *American Negro Folktales.* New York: Fawcett Premier Books, 1956.

Douglass, Frederick. *Narrative of the Life of Frederick Douglass: An American Slave, Written by Himself.* New York: Signet, 1968.

Georgia Writers' Project. *Drums and Shadows: Survival Studies among the Georgia Coastal Negroes.* Athens, GA: University of Georgia Press, 1940.

Goodell, William. *The American Slave Code in Theory and Practice: Its Distinctive Features Shown by Its Statutes, Judicial Decisions, and Illustrative Facts.* New York: American and Foreign Anti-Slavery Society, 1853. http://www.dinsdoc.com/goodell-1-1-11.htm.

Hughes, Langston, and Arna Bontemps, eds. *The Book of Negro Folklore.* New York: Dodd Mead & Co., 1958.

Jones, Charles C. Jr. *Negro Myths from the Georgia Coast Told in the Vernacular.* Boston and New York: Houghton, Mifflin & Co., 1888.

Larson, Kate Clifford. *Bound for the Promised Land: Harriet Tubman: Portrait of an American Hero.* New York: Ballantine Books, 2003.

Lester, Julius. *To Be a Slave.* New York, Dial Book, 1998.

Lyons, Mary. *Letters from a Slave Girl, by Harriet Jacobs.* New York: Simon & Schuster, 1992.

Still, William. *Underground Railroad: A Record of Facts, Authentic Narratives, etc.* Philadelphia: Porter and Coales, Publishers, 1872. http://www.msa.md.gov/megafile/msa/speccol/sc5300/sc5339/000047/000000/000001/restricted/l1117/html/031645-0000.html.

Stowe, Harriet Beecher. *Uncle Tom's Cabin.* New York: Modern Library, 1996.

• Websites •

America's Library. "African-American Folk Artist Harriet Powers Was Born October 29, 1837." Accessed March 24, 2009. http://www.americaslibrary.gov/jb/reform/jb_reform_powers_1.html.

Archer Collection, The. "The History of Teaching Literacy." San Francisco State University Leonard Library. Accessed November 20, 2009. http://www.library.sfsu.edu/about/collections/archer/history-teach.html.

Chronicling America. "The National Era." The Library of Congress: National Endowment for the Humanities. Accessed August 20, 2007. http://chroniclingamerica.loc.gov/lccn/sn84026752/.

EyeWitness to History. "Life on a Southern Plantation, 1854." Accessed August 27, 2007. http://www.eyewitnesstohistory.com/plantation.htm.

General Records of the United States. "The Emancipation Proclamation." United States National Archives & Records Administration. Accessed October 23, 2009. http://www.archives.gov/exhibits/featured_documents/emancipation_proclamation/index.html.

Ham, Debra Newman. "Free Blacks in Maryland." In Maryland Online Encyclopedia. Maryland Historical Society, the Maryland Humanities Council, the Enoch Pratt Free Library, and the Maryland State Department of Education, 2004–2005. http://www.mdoe.org/freeblacksinmd.html.

Harriet Tubman Staff. "Harriet Tubman Special Resource Study Project." National Park Service U.S. Department of the Interior. Last modified March 17, 2009. http://www.harriettubmanstudy.org/index.htm.

Ives, Sarah. "*Did Quilts Hold Codes to the Underground Railroad?*" National Geographic News, February 5, 2004. http://news.nationalgeographic.com/news/2004/02/0205_040205_slavequilts.html.

John W. Jones Museum, The. "The John W. Jones Museum website." Accessed October 27, 2009. http://www.johnwjonesmuseum.org/.

Jones, Christopher, and Roger Turner. "Exploring Illness Across Time and Place." The University of Pennsylvania. Accessed August 8, 2007. http://www.sas.upenn.edu/~rogert/19wv.html.

Lamb, Annette, and Larry Johnson. Updated by Nancy Smith. "Underground Railroad." 42eXplore: Thematic Pathfinders for All Ages. Last modified September 2002. http://www.42explore2.com/undergrd.htm.

Library of Congress, The. "Born in Slavery: Slave Narratives from the Federal Writer's Project, 1936–1938." The Library of Congress American Memory Collection. Last modified March 23, 2001. http://memory.loc.gov/ammem/snhtml/snhome.html.

Maryland Historical Society. "African Americans in the Maritime Trades." Accessed June 20, 2008. http://www.mdhs.org/learn_afam_mari_trade_lesson.html.

Maryland Public Television. "Pathways to Freedom: Maryland and the Underground Railroad." Accessed February 11, 2007. http://pathways.thinkport.org/static_home.cfm.

National Humanities Center. "Timeline: 1800–1860." Toolbox Library: Primary Resources in U.S. History and Literature. Accessed August 7, 2008. http://nationalhumanitiescenter.org/pds/triumphnationalism/timeline.pdf.

National Park Service. "National Underground Railroad Network to Freedom Listings." U.S. Department of the Interior. Last modified September 12, 2008. http://www.nps.gov/history/ugrr/list.htm.